Delirium Eclipse
&Other
Stories

Delirium Eclipse
&Other Stories

James Lasdun

1817
HARPER & ROW, PUBLISHERS, New York
Cambridge, Philadelphia, San Francisco, London
Mexico City, São Paulo, Singapore, Sydney

The following stories in the collection have appeared previously: "Property" *(Encounter)*; "The Siege" *(Cosmopolitan)*; "Dead Labor" *(Fiction Magazine)*; "The Spoiling" *(Firebird 1*, published by Penguin Books, Ltd.); "The Bugle" *(Literary Review)*; "Delirium Eclipse" *(Woman's Journal)*.

This collection was published in Great Britain under the title *The Silver Age.*

FIRST U.S. EDITION

Designer: Jénine Holmes

Library of Congress Cataloging-in-Publication Data

Lasdun, James.
    Delirium eclipse and other stories.

    Contents: Delirium eclipse—Property—The siege—[etc.]
    I. Title.
PR6062.A735D4   1986   823'.914   85-45644
ISBN 0-06-015550-7

86 87 88 89 90 HC 10 9 8 7 6 5 4 3 2 1

Contents

Delirium Eclipse

L EWIS JACKSON HAD about ten million dollars of multi-national aid at his disposal. It was a large sum for a man as young as himself to be tending, but he was properly aware of his responsibilities, and confident in his ability to shoulder them.

His ascent through the hierarchies of his career had been rapid and smooth. His still-boyish face was glazed with the patina acquired by people who work in the medium of success. He now found himself representing quite a substantial node in the planet's economic grid, and he could feel the hum of power in his veins.

His assignment—the first serious one he had been given—was in the south of India, where he was to budget the finances for a series of projects ranging from the sinking of village wells to the planting and irrigation of thousands of hectares of new orchards.

There were six weeks to go before he was due to begin, and he decided to fill the interval by visiting the great Mogul sites in the north of the country.

Shortly before he left, he met a girl called Clare at a party in a Kilburn squat. They could see the bronze glitter of the canal from the window where they stood. The brick houses facing it were sepia in the lamplight, and the sky was violet.

"Imagine if that canal was the river Ganges, and those

3

houses were temples," was Jackson's opening line, after which he was able to steer the conversation quite naturally around to his ten million dollars and his projects. He spoke of peaches, plums, mangoes, and limes, of fungicides and fertilizers, of crop yields waiting to be multiplied tenfold or more. . . . His eloquence was lit up with the immediacy of personal involvement, so that even if Clare wasn't interested in the subject matter, she couldn't help noticing the energy with which it was communicated, and this energy drew her toward him.

She was carefree, relaxed, and quite without guile. She lived on the dole, and spent her time at the dance, language, and craft classes her local council provided for its unemployed, at a nominal fee.

Her hair was a very shiny gold on the top, but increasingly dark toward its roots—burnt stubble colors. It was thick and unkempt, and hung in a tea-towel girdle like a sheaf of wheat. Her eyes were a pale slate color when looked at; a perfect blue when remembered. Her face was broad and strong, but also faintly childish in a Nordic way. It looked well accustomed to expressing pleasure, and little else. A Kirlian photograph of her would have revealed a brilliant aura burning about her body like Saint Elmo's fire, indicative of unusual spiritual and physical vigor.

Within minutes of meeting her, Jackson had set his heart on taking her with him to India. There was some urgency, for he intended leaving in a few days, but as he unfurled before her his visions of plenty, he felt certain that whatever it would take of charm, cunning, and willpower to persuade her to come, he possessed it in abundance. He felt invincible. In the event, the only serious obstacle he had to overcome was her reluctance to let him pay her way, she having no money of her own. She allowed herself to be swayed when he told her how much he was being paid, and hinted at the latitude of his expense allowance. It was as much the spontaneity of the idea that appealed to her as its promise of adventure, and having agreed to it, she couldn't wait to go. Jackson congratulated himself on his good fortune in finding a traveling companion as pleasant and equable as Clare, though he didn't doubt he deserved it.

Pearl mosques, incense, cane juice, desert forts, the deft hands of itinerant foot masseurs, the unearthly sound of vultures at carrion . . . They traveled in a leisurely way, stopping for everything.

They enjoyed each other's company. Clare, a natural hedonist and libertine, was content to focus the entire range of her sensuality on Jackson alone, which made him feel like a prince. His health was so good that he soon gave up dissolving chlorine tablets in his water, and joined Clare, who disdained such precautions, in drinking from the tap. He was in fine, magnanimous humor. He scattered coins before beggars, gave liberal tips to rickshaw drivers, and patronized street vendors avidly, accumulating garlands of colorful bead necklaces, shiny silk scarves, and innumerable little trinkets, decking Clare out in increasingly sumptuous combinations of his purchases.

The closest they came to a quarrel was outside the Red Fort at Agra, where Jackson wrote a warm, witty postcard to someone whom he had only that morning described to Clare in terms of the most crushing contempt. Clare colored as she read it.

"You shouldn't send that," she said.

"Why on earth not?"

"It's hypocritical."

Jackson told her not to be so silly, but she persisted in a slow, painfully obstinate way. "I wish you'd tear it up," she said, and, "I would never send a postcard like that to someone I despised."

Finally, Jackson snapped at her: "If you attach your integrity to something as trivial as a postcard, then it can't be worth much. I reserve mine for more important things."

She recoiled into a puzzled, hurt silence, while Jackson went off to buy a stamp.

He was pleased with his retort; at first because it seemed so clever, and then because it began to seem true. It crystallized the Jesuitical sense he had that the gravity of his work licensed him to trade with impunity in the sort of deceptions Clare objected to. A mission to irrigate orchards guaranteed your soul against damage from these minor acts of dissembling. If anything, the more you exposed yourself to them, the stronger your conviction was proved to be. Reaching that conclusion, Jackson felt a twinge of pity for Clare, who had nothing weightier in her life than the sincerity of her postcards against which to measure herself. He bought a sapphire from a gem hawker outside the post office, and gave it to Clare when he got back to the tea stall where she was waiting for him.

"There you are," he said, "that's what I call an important thing."

She looked at him warily, uncertain whether to believe him. He faced her with his most unflinchingly honest gaze. As he watched her gradually giving him the benefit of the doubt, he felt a curious, complex sensation of joy: he had made her believe the sapphire was a token of love, which it wasn't, by sheer force of will, and it gratified him to see that he possessed this power. But simultaneously, the sight of Clare *accepting* it as a token of love gave him a rush of the kind of elated yearning he had only previously felt for complete strangers—beautiful women at airports or concerts, whom he would never talk to and never see again. . . . To feel like that about a girl who was looking at him as lovingly as Clare was now, whom if he wanted he could take back to their room this minute and ravish, was blissful.

Mr. Birla, the manager of their hotel in the holy city of Varanasi, was a friendly young man dressed in jeans and a tight floral shirt. He spoke English well, and informed them he was an Anglophile. He said he had a stock list of English delicacies which he was working through alphabetically. Last month his kitchen had been filled with boxes of lime cordial, lemon curd, and luncheon meat. This month it was marmalade, muffins, macaroons, malt loaf, and Marmite. He sincerely hoped they would not feel homesick.

He showed them to a room with a small balcony from which they could just see the far shore of a massive brown tract of water, calm beneath an oily haze: the river Ganges.

He said they had arrived on a very important day. There was to be a partial eclipse of the sun that afternoon, an event of great significance in the Hindu calendar. There would be processions along the river, chanting, "all these kind of things." He offered to accompany them.

The streets were already beginning to swarm as they set off. Sadhus were striding about singing and praying. A Mercedes van with smoked-glass windows pulled up on one street and disgorged a dozen pink-skinned devotees of Krishna, who danced off like fully wound-up clockwork toys, banging cymbals and drums, and singing their song. Here and there they or the sadhus sent a charge of fervor rippling through the crowds gathering around them, though it was still a tentative, experimental fervor, and a man seized by it one minute might easily break off to buy a popadum or a cup of hot spiced milk the next.

Everyone was making for the great stone steps that led down to the Ganges. These were carpeted with people, milling, jostling, weaving about in processions. . . .

Jackson could see that Clare was already entering into the spirit of the occasion. A look of delight was fixed on her broad, healthy face. She beamed at everyone who passed. An old crone, muttering an incantation, was reeling from person to person, anointing foreheads with greasepaint. Mr. Birla saw her off with a little gesture of disdain. Jackson followed suit. But Clare solemnly parted her hair and lowered her head toward the woman, rising again with a smudge of red above her eyebrows. "Who was she?" she whispered to Mr. Birla. "Holy woman," he answered, in a matter-of-fact voice. Clare looked exultant. A moment later she was caught in a crush of human traffic. She rose a few inches into the air, and glided along, borne by the pressure of the crowd. She turned round to look at Jackson, shaking the dark golden mass of her hair out of her eyes. She was smiling rapturously at him. As he smiled back, Jackson's heart swelled with pride, as if he himself had conjured this radiant creature into being.

They were down at the river now. Rowboats tethered to jetties jostled each other in the brown water. People were swimming and washing themselves. Jackson could see trickles of effluvia, glistening like snail tracks, dribbling into the water. Right beside him, a boy was washing a herd of water buffalo in the shallows, scraping the matted dung off their rears, scrubbing their dusty black hides until they looked Brylcreem-slick, and the sunlight made a blue gleam on the cusp of each muscle corrugation in their necks.

A surge of noise, cymbals crashing, drums . . . Something happened to the daylight. It didn't darken so much as distort. The whole dome of sky was like an eye being squeezed askew. Jackson could hear a roaring, but far away; he was fixed in the space immediately about him, as if in bending it had become vitreous—a great glass orb. He squinted up at the sun: quartz-cold brilliance. "Do not look at the sun," he heard Mr. Birla say. It cut a glittering trail of light across his vision as he turned away; coruscating, like diamond dust. For an instant he was snow-blind, his insides curling from some obscure discomfort. The sun had been misshapen. He had the impression of having seen a scimitar edge of absolute blackness probing into it—a tiny penetration of darkness into the source of light itself.

On the way back to their hotel, they passed the general post office, which Jackson had given as a *poste restante* to his employers and family, should they wish to contact him. Leaving Clare with Mr. Birla, he went in to see if there was anything waiting for him. A telegram was eventually handed over the counter. He tore it open. "Agency closing down. Funds transferred. All projects cancelled. All staff kaput. Please no more expenses. Will explain on your return."

He sat down on a bench at the back of the stuffy, paper-strewn room, breathing deeply, to regain his composure. He was acutely conscious of the fatigue of his body, which flushed all over like a fanned ember when he looked at the telegram again. When he could, he stood up and walked slowly toward the exit. On his way out, he crumpled up the telegram and threw it into a bin.

"Anything?" Clare asked.

"No. Nothing at all."

The following morning Jackson's eyes were ablaze with conjunctivitis. Scarlet threads of vein straggled out from each canthus toward the pupil. His eyeballs felt as if they'd been doused in acid. He smeared them with Chloromycetin ointment from a tube in his washbag. As he looked at himself in the mirror, he flinched, as if he had seen not himself but some unsavory acquaintance from long ago in the past, who was swimming up to him, grinning like a blackmailer.

"Don't even think about it," Clare whispered, kissing his eyelids. "It'll soon disappear." He said as little as possible to her; he was still trying to calculate how much of his news he could conceal from her, and how she would react to what he chose to reveal.

They walked down to the river, Jackson's eyes streaming behind a pair of sunglasses. There was a bitterness at the back of his throat, where some of the ointment, diluted by tears, had trickled down his sinuses.

They had planned to swim, but when they actually reached the river, Jackson began to have doubts. He could see one of the snail trails of sewage he had observed the day before, trickling into the water. There was a smell of barbecued meat on the air from the Burning Ghats, where corpses were cremated on wooden pyres, their ashes sent floating out onto the river on little rafts.

He had read the passage in the guidebook describing the miraculous medicinal properties attributed to the Ganges; tests—"scientific tests"—had shown that water from cholera-ridden tributaries was purified within seconds of its penetrating the holy river. The time when these myths would have sufficed, and he would have plunged in without hesitation, already seemed remote from him.

"You go in. I'll wait here with the things."

Dressed in a blue swimsuit, Clare stepped down through the sandy mud to the river. Her skin looked very dusky in the gloom afforded by Jackson's sunglasses. She waded into the water, splashing it on her waist and shoulders before kicking herself free of the ground and plunging in. She swam out from the shore, covering yards with each thrust of her strong arms and legs. Her body churned the water into bronze scoops and billows that fanned out behind her, tiger-striping the surface with big ripples. Jackson watched her, his mind a jumble of desire and misgivings: the free abandon with which she plunged and twisted in the water had in it something distantly threatening as well as graceful. A dangerous self-sufficiency. Perhaps after all he ought to join her in the water; it might make her less likely to suspect there was anything seriously the matter with him.

He stripped to his trunks and stepped gingerly down to the river. He felt peculiarly naked and vulnerable, as if he had taken off not only his clothes but also a layer of skin, and there was now nothing between his internal organs and the water. Clare waved, and called to him. She was a good thirty yards out. He could hardly retreat now. Goosebumps swarmed over his back and shoulders. The water was warm and thick with detritus. His toes sank deep into the soft riverbed. He kicked free and started to swim toward Clare. Something solid bobbed against his thigh. A fish, he tried to think, but could only imagine human excrement, or charred human remains; a burnt hand touching his thigh, a blackened tongue . . . An involuntary spasm quivered through him, and he panicked, jackknifing around, thrashing wildly at the water in his haste to get out. Quite soon he was shivering.

He lay alone on the sagging double bed. That morning he had taken his temperature, and sent the silver thread straight up to a hundred and two.

Clare was with Mr. Birla, who had invited them to visit his family's carpet factory that day. She had offered to stay behind with Jackson, but he could see she wanted to go, and although he would have preferred not to lose sight of her, he decided there was less to be lost by a show of carefree acquiescence than one of possessiveness.

He was in quite a bad way. There was a fever ache in his bones, and dysentery in his bowels. His eyes were still so inflamed that direct sunlight caused him unbearable pain. The curtains were shut, the dark room stifling. Now and then he had to drag himself upstairs to squat at the cracked and stinking porcelain throat that connected the hotel with the river. He voided himself there with a ferocity that left him shattered. He was in a groggy, twilit stupor of aspirin, streptomycin, and Chloromycetin. Thoughts drifted through him, but he hadn't the energy to seize hold of one for more than a few seconds. They slipped by, inconclusively. The telegram had blown him wide open. He didn't know what to do. He wondered what the matter with him was; he seemed to have lost all his power of resistance. Clare wasn't getting ill. Had her life provided her with some crucial immunity that his own had not? He remembered himself as a schoolboy: shy, insecure, unaccustomed to attention, deeply affected by it when it came his way. A washroom surrounded with mirrors . . . Someone teasing him for his baby face . . . He'd blushed with pleasure as the insults flew at him. Nothing like this had happened to him before; he was being celebrated, never mind why. He started laughing wildly, braying. He could see himself in the mirrors. His face was incapable of expressing so much ecstasy, and it began to twist and curl in all the wrong ways, absolutely out of control. Finally tears started pouring down his cheeks—"It's all right," he sobbed, "I'm still laughing, I'm still laughing," and the place had frozen up in an embarrassed silence. . . . It was that schoolboy's face he had seen in the mirror yesterday morning. What is wrong with me? The question hung in abeyance. He was sleepy by the time Clare returned.

She was in a jubilant mood: "What a place!"

She whisked open the curtains, letting in a bright sunbeam that hit Jackson's eyes like a punch.

"Don't."

Instead of closing the curtains, she picked up Jackson's sunglasses and stuck them on his face. "There we are. No need for Clare to sit in darkness all afternoon, is there?" She kissed him on the forehead. She had never babied him before, and the unprecedented tone had a faintly depressing effect on him.

"There were huge copper vats full of dye, and bales of thread the most gorgeous colors stacked all over the place. And then these little children, tiny little things, just everywhere, little mice . . ." She giggled. "They get four rupees a day, which Shiva says is a fortune for them—"

"Shiva?"

"Mr. Birla. He's a lovely man. . . . I told him all about your projects. He'd love to talk to you. . . . I said you'd like that too and he could come up anytime. He took me into a room completely covered with the carpets they make. I wish I could describe them to you. . . ." She attempted, and even though she stumbled clumsily from one superlative to another, her words worked on Jackson's drowsy imagination to produce an impression of bright patterns, stylized animals, birds, flowers, all glimmering through a medium of peacock plumage alloyed with silver and mother-of-pearl. She was more than usually voluble; the place had evidently had an effect on her.

"The best thing was how they were made—you'd've adored it, Lewis. Half a dozen of these toddlers sit in a pile of thread weavering away like mad, with an old man beside them just singing, and the thing was that what he sang was the pattern of the carpet, which was how the children knew what to do. What they wove depended on what he sang. Do you see? Isn't that good? The carpet is a song turned into a silk tapestry. Lewis? Lewis?" She lowered her voice to a whisper. "Are you awake?"

"Hm."

How tired he felt. He yawned. He could hardly hear what Clare was saying. Was she saying anything now? A hand touched his forehead. His various discomforts floated away just far enough to let his mind relax its vigil over his body. . . .

He woke up at dusk, his head reverberating with an absurd dream phrase spoken in Clare's voice: "Shivaring away like mad." She wasn't in the room. His sunglasses had been placed on the bedside table, on top of a note. "Back soon."

He wondered what she could be doing. An idea came to him: she was downstairs having sex with Mr. Birla. He sent it packing. He wished he could read a book, or get up and go for a walk. He turned over the bolster and straightened the sheet on top of him. He could feel the idea hovering in the wings. Shivaring away like mad. Resist it, he told himself. He tried to think of something else. Nothing. A pulse of alarm struck up beneath his ribs. An image of Clare and Mr. Birla locked together in a naked embrace blossomed in his mind like a big pink and brown flower. He winced, shook his head. But there was nothing between him and the idea. He seemed to have as little immunity to it as he had against the microbes swarming in his body. Here was Clare again. It was like a film, a conscientiously scrupulous pornographic film. He sat up and tried to block it out by reciting the only thing he knew by heart, which was the Lord's Prayer. Our Father which art in heaven, Hallowed be Thy name . . . but there was Clare sighing while Mr. Birla's fingers slid under her loose silk shirt to fondle her breasts. . . . Thy kingdom come. Thy will be done, on earth as it is in heaven. Give us this day . . . and Mr. Birla was underneath her while she slid the cushioned chassis of her hips to and fro astride him, a flush of pink washing her body. . . . Jackson sat up appalled. A cold veil of sweat surfaced on his brow. Give us this day our daily bread and forgive us our trespasses; as we . . . and there were two Mr. Birlas now, one of them calmly fucking Clare from behind, the other stroking the golden hair buried in his groin. Why is this happening to me, Jackson thought. He did not want to see these things.

He looked around the shadowy room for something to distract himself with. The room service buzzer . . . If he pressed it and Mr. Birla came up within . . . within a minute, that would bring an end to these anxieties. He pressed it.

Mr. Birla arrived with such alacrity that Jackson hadn't even begun to think what he would actually say to him. But he was spared the trouble by Mr. Birla himself.

"Hello," the summoned manager said. "I was just thinking of popping up and looking in. How are your spirits?"

He hardly looked like a cuckold-maker—tight polka-dot shirt shadowed at the hollows of his bony shoulders and collarbone, a crumbling battlement of dentistry silhouetted in his grin.

"I'm all right, thanks," Jackson said, feeling a little relieved.

"Oh, good." Mr. Birla stepped right inside the room. "I understand you are engaged on important business. Distributing welfare, is it?" He half *v*'d the *w* of welfare, and concluded with a charming smile, eager for conversation.

"Oh, yes. That's right," Jackson said. Now of course it was necessary to get rid of the man. "I wondered, actually, could I . . ." Inspiration struck him: "Could you bring me some muffins, please, with marmalade, and Marmite?"

Mr. Birla looked momentarily startled. His smile went glassy as he reverted from would-be conversationalist to hotel manager.

"Of course," he said. "Thank you."

Clare had been swimming. She came back with wet hair, and hung her costume up to dry.

Like his dysentery, Jackson's feelings of jealousy were tidal. They could ebb so far away that they would seem no more than a vague, dispersed nightmare. But when they rose, they engulfed him, and this they tended to do whenever Clare went out. Within minutes of her departure, her blithe, relaxed manner began to curdle in Jackson's memory. He realized her poise was a sham, performed in order to quell precisely the suspicions he was harboring. The realization coexisted with a full awareness that it was groundless, but this didn't in the least diminish its effects. His imagination began to seethe, his fever to rise; he would start trembling and sweating. Finally he would hit the room service buzzer, summoning Mr. Birla, whom he would scrutinize with increasingly blatant hostility before ordering a plate of macaroons, or a muffin, or a slice of malt loaf. An incidental benefit of this procedure was that it supplied Jackson with nourishment bland enough for him to consume: he had come to regard eating Indian food as a form of Russian roulette, where every mouthful might be loaded. He had lost his taste for it.

The frequency with which he summoned Mr. Birla increased rapidly. Soon he had him running up and down stairs five or six times a morning. By then he hardly knew why he did it, but it satisfied him in an obscure way to exercise the power. "Thank you," Mr. Birla always said when Jackson finally snapped his order at him. He didn't try to engage Jackson in conversation again.

Meanwhile Jackson was growing steadily more ill. His eyes were swollen and rheumy. He developed a streaming cold. A small colony of itchy red spots between his toes ran riot, covering both feet with a livid, burning rash. He lay all day in shadow. Sometimes he would be aware of Clare lying beside him, talking about her day, cooling his forehead with a flannel. Then somehow she would have vanished, and in no time Jackson would have to hit the room service buzzer again. . . .

One day she produced from her bag a bottle of Dr. Collis Brown—an opium-based panacea which she had discovered in the bathroom cupboard of her squat. It was the only medicine she had brought.

"Why don't we try this for a change?" She poured out a spoonful for Jackson. It was sweet and fiery.

"Maybe I'll have some too." She took a swig straight from the bottle, and passed the bottle back to Jackson, smiling mischievously. "Go on. . . ." By the time they had finished it, Jackson was feeling a pleasant, slightly drunken sensation. Clare snuggled up next to him on the bed. Her bushy hair brushed against his skin, and set him tingling. He was floating, immensely happy. A lot of time went by very quickly, or else a little, slowly. His body wasn't hurting at all. He plied his fingers through Clare's hair. A rustle like a breeze through copper-colored leaves . . . Tiny golden sparks began to tumble out of it with each stroke. The more he brushed the brighter they grew, and when he stopped they faded.

"Are you seeing things too?" Clare asked in a faraway voice.

"Oh, yes . . . so I am. . . ."

They lay still. He was in a room like this but different. Clare was kneeling by the bed.

"Look," she said, placing a hand on each side of her head. "Look . . ." She lifted away the top of her head. Jackson peered over: a crystalline, miniature landscape . . . mountains with snow and dark green pines. Still blue lakes, and on a far shore an icy blue sea with motionless white crests . . .

"Now you . . ." she said. But he was looking at the wall. There was a hole in it he hadn't seen before, with a bird's nest inside. A spider the size of a hand was sitting on the twigs, its black head probing down into the broken shell of a pale blue egg. A bead of golden yolk was sliding down the side of the shell. "Make me come," he heard Clare whisper. She was naked, aroused. Her breasts had turned a rosy color at their tips. She pressed them to his face and wrapped her legs around him. "Come on . . ."

"Look at the spider," Jackson said. It took him hours to form the syllables. She knelt up slowly on the bed and leaned toward it. As she did so, the bird's nest disappeared, and the hole shrank to a shallow cavity of flaked-away plaster. There was no trace of the egg or its liquid treasure. "Sweet little spider." She reached her hand toward it and picked it up very gently by one leg. It wriggled, grappling with the air close to Clare's naked skin. Jackson had to close his eyes for a moment. When he opened them again she was at the window talking to the spider, wishing it a pleasant journey to the ground. It was much smaller than he had imagined. "Bye, bye, little spider," Clare said. She drifted back to bed and covered Jackson's face with kisses. He rolled away. "Don't feel like it," he said. "Sleep."

It was evening. Beyond the window the dark pink sunset was drawn, like a conjuror's silk handkerchief, through a band of clouds, from which it emerged a watery blue. Jackson stretched and sat up. He could feel the imprint of the sweaty, crumpled linen on his cheeks. Clare wasn't there. He had no idea when he had last seen her.

There was something on the floor by the bed. Jackson peered down, touched it.

It was a rolled-up carpet about six feet in width. He stared at it a moment, wondering where it had come from. Clare couldn't possibly have afforded to buy a carpet with the pocket money he gave her, and he was certain she had no secret stash of her own. He checked his own wallet; nothing was missing. How had she got hold of it? It must have been a gift. Jackson felt the familiar signals of alarm go off in his body. He pressed the buzzer. A minute went by, two minutes. He pressed it again. An old woman he hadn't seen before finally appeared, wheezing and dragging her feet. She tilted her chin at Jackson, questioningly.

"Mr. Birla?" he asked. She shook her finger and gestured with it toward the window: gone out. Jackson thanked her, and she shuffled off.

He lay back on the bed with a feeling of acute consternation. He told himself over and over that there was absolutely no basis for his anxieties; and meanwhile he grew quite frantic. Images of Clare and Mr. Birla played in his mind with the intensity of an hallucination. He had nothing to fight them with, and they took on a life of their own, commandeering his imagination, like the amoebas in his bowels. He started shaking. Fever flushes rushed through his body. The intensity and luridness of his imaginings proliferated until he began to feel he was losing his grip. He had to move.

He climbed out of bed and put on a pair of light cotton pajamas. His legs were wobbly from lack of use, though this had the effect of making him feel oddly light rather than heavy. He took his wallet and documents so that he could leave the door unlocked in case Clare came back before him. The evening light being just tolerable, he left his sunglasses behind. The old woman was sitting at Mr. Birla's desk in the lobby. She looked at him impassively as he stumbled by her, out onto the street.

After a few yards he was panting; he was in no condition to be out. He waved down a bicycle rickshaw and climbed into the chariot-like seat. They rumbled over the cobbles, into the maze of alleys that led down the steps.

The city was coming to life as the day cooled. People were out strolling. The street markets, some of them already lit with kerosene lamps, were trading busily. There was food everywhere. There seemed to be a surplus of it. Unwanted mangoes and limes lay in broken crates outside shops, fermenting into chutney; Jackson could smell the sweet syrup odor of fruit rot as he went by. Apple scab, he remembered from his training, potato canker, honey fungus, white rot, black rust . . . Pomegranates and papayas tumbled from overladen stalls onto the cobbles, where their heedless owners watched them disappear into the mitts of furtive monkeys. A skew-horned cow patrolling one of the alleys dragged, like a prisoner's ball, a giant watermelon she had stamped on, and which no one had troubled to prize from her hoof. There was meat in abundance too—garroted guinea fowl, skinned lambs dressed in living fleeces of big black flies, goats' heads, foamy swathes of what looked like, but surely could not have been, tripe still green with cud. . . . Jackson watched a beggar tip ruefully from his brass bowl a mound of sticky rice that even his elastic appetite had been unable to accommodate. There were smells of cooking in the air—garlic and coriander, spice smells of cardamom and cinnamon, acrid odors from the dung-burning stoves over which soot-blackened vats simmered and steamed, and floating over these, the soapy smells of incense, frangipani, sandalwood. . . .

Too much was going on. Radios and klaxons were blaring out, flutes, drums, voices. . . . There were too many people and the rickshaw driver kept stopping to let them pass in front of him. Dogs and monkeys were rooting in the gutters. Cows choked up the alleys until they felt like ambling on. Jackson had an urgent desire to get down to the river. It made him feel uncomfortable to dawdle among all this plenty. He felt lost and insignificant. "I'm in rather a hurry," he said to the rickshaw driver, who smiled and said nothing. They were hardly moving. Come on, come on, Jackson thought. "Come on," he shouted. He could see knotted veins bulging like worm casts on the driver's skinny calves. Looking at them he had a brief intimation that if he'd had a whip, he would have used it. His fever was running high.

It was almost dark by the time they reached the steps that led down to the river. Fires were burning here and there, and the level sun made the sullage in the water look like gold dust. The steps were staggered, uneven, muddied by a mulch of crushed marigolds and rose petals. The whole higgledy-piggledy embankment with its crooked paths and terraced buildings stacked precariously on top of each other, saris flapping on the vast web of lines stretched between them, was more like vegetation than carefully assembled stone. The budding tip of a new shrine pushing its way through a crack in the ground would not have been an altogether surprising sight. Jackson climbed down, scanning the water for Clare. He was in a particular state of mind that internalizes everything perceived, giving it the viscosity of a dream landscape—temples flowed past him, people in prayer or meditation dissolved into the glare of torch-light, shadowy figures swam into focus and then ceased to exist. His head was throbbing. The steps seemed end-less and unreal.

He was still some way from the water when a head of fair hair rose up from it, followed by a body in a dark blue swimsuit. Before the body had reached full height, the head of hair had already bushed out from its water-sleeked anonymity and taken on a burnish of firelight. Water streamed from the body, draping it for a second like a glassy dress; leaving behind a few beads in which the last of the light took refuge. . . . She walked slowly out of the water, smiling faintly to herself. Jackson stayed very still. He felt invisible. He watched her stoop for her towel and hold it round herself with one hand, while with the other she slid the swimsuit from her body. She knelt down to dry herself. There was nothing but twilight between her nakedness and the eyes of people wandering by the river. She was oblivious. She dried herself slowly and carefully, luxuriating, it seemed, in the sensations of her body. She put on a dress and strolled toward the steps, several yards along from where Jackson stood.

He hung back, following her from a short distance, half-thinking Mr. Birla was suddenly going to appear at her side, half-knowing he would not.

A figure approached her from the shadows . . . not Mr. Birla, but a leper hobbling on a pair of makeshift crutches tied under his shoulders. His feet were ban-daged in rags and his skin was mottled like a wall with bad damp. There was a box hanging from his neck. Clare fumbled in her purse for coins, which she held out to him at arm's length. The leper stood still with his head bowed as she dropped the coins in his box. From where

Jackson stood, along the steps, he could see it dawning on Clare that the man had interpreted her outstretched arm as a sign that he was to come no closer. A look of anxiety at her unintended coldness crossed her face as the leper thanked her and turned to go. "Oh . . . wait." She put her hand on his shoulder to detain him, and as he heaved himself back round on his crutches, she ran her fingers lightly down his arm, resting her hand a moment on his scabbed stump. The leper stood obediently still while Clare stared at him, her mouth open as if she were on the point of uttering some phrase that would magic away his disease. Then, remembering herself, she dug into her purse again, taking out not coins, but something that sparkled as she dropped it into the box: the sapphire Jackson had given her.

Jackson watched it all with a feeling of vertiginous wonder. What was he to make of this? There was too much new, bewildering information crammed into Clare's gestures and actions for him to comprehend it all at once. It was like being dazzled by a glare. As he watched her disappear into the dark city, he realized he had seriously underestimated her. There was a side to her he had failed to appreciate. Her uncomplicatedness wasn't the same as simplicity: he had glimpsed behind it, into a world where his own labyrinthine relations with people and possessions had no place, where you gave and took as you felt like or needed, and that was that. He walked back slowly, feeling faintly ashamed of his furtive behavior, and trying to assess how much damage it had done. He resolved never to indulge his suspicions again, and as he did so, it occurred to him that the only probable explanation for the presence of the carpet in their room was that Clare had borrowed it, just so that she could show him one. How extraordinarily thoughtful she was. He felt like someone coming out of a delirium: feeling his way back along a frail vein of reality. And it was the way back to health too; all he had to do was concentrate on holding on.

There was no one at the desk when he reentered the hotel. He climbed up the stairs, feeling rather stronger on his legs than he had when he'd set out. I'm recovering, he told himself, and felt an anticipatory buzz of well-being. The dimly lit staircase smelled of stale incense and drains: not a place he would be sorry to leave. There was enough money left for another week or so. They could go somewhere they hadn't planned to visit: Assam perhaps, or Kashmir, hire a wooden houseboat on Lake Srinagar—mountains and snow, lush valleys. . . . There was time to make a fresh start. He would tell her about the agency closing down; she wouldn't give a damn. He'd pretend he'd just been down to the post office, and found the telegram.

The light was on, peeping under the door, but the door was locked. He rattled the handle. "It's me." Scuffling sounds, a delay. "Open up, it's me." Clare opened the door: "Oh, there you are. Where on earth have you been? We thought you'd been kidnapped." Mr. Birla was in the room. Jackson stepped inside, screwing up his eyes against the electric light. He looked at Clare, and at Mr. Birla. Clare was talking breathlessly. "Did you see this carpet Shiva gave us?" he heard her say. "Isn't it beautiful? Look—" She knelt down and began to unroll it. Flowers and grasses appeared, tree trunks, boughs, foliage. . . . Jackson stared at it intently while Clare went on talking: "Have you ever seen anything so lovely . . ." A dizzy feeling went through him as he tried to resist wondering why the door had been locked, why Mr. Birla was there, and why Clare was talking so wildly. Bright

lemons and limes hung between the leaves on the carpet, and on one tree there were big lustrous peaches,
shaded at the cleft and toned miraculously through from
yellow to scarlet. "A small gift," Mr. Birla said. Jackson
peered even closer as Mr. Birla edged behind him toward
the door. He noticed how the leaves were individually
veined, how some were curled to show a paler reverse,
how there was even a silvery down of furze visible on the
peaches if you looked carefully. "I have received my new
shipment," Mr. Birla was saying as he backed into the
corridor. "Nesquik, Nutella, a box of nougat—I'll bring
you some nougat." Then Clare stepped forward with his
sunglasses. "There's too much light in here," she said,
"it's too bright for you. You'll damage yourself." She
stuck them on his face and went out, saying she'd be
back in a while, that she wouldn't be long.

Property

A SMALL PARCEL arrived on the first morning of my visit
to my grandmother at her flat in Mayfair. I watched
her opening it amid the debris of our breakfast. The
process was very slow and laborious; her fingers were
gnarled and weakened by arthritis, and could barely gain
sufficient purchase to loosen the bow, let alone break
the string. The sight of those hands, I remember, was
like a dream of helplessness; it sapped all the strength
from me. She tried, and failed, and tried again to slip the
slackened cradle of string around the edge of the little
box. A small cluster of rubies nestled beneath a knuckle,
as startling there as the tiny brilliant cherries that sometimes appear on trees in derelict orchards. The back of
each hand was mottled with purple veins and mauve
contusions.

Inside the parcel was a pair of ornate silver scissors
with a little box protruding from the blades. It was for
snuffing candles. My grandmother held the scissors at
arm's length, peered at them, and then gave a soft cry of
recognition. There was a note with them, which she
read, also at arm's length.

"How very peculiar." She passed the note to me.

"Dear Mrs. Cranbourne," it read. "I am returning
these candle-trimmers which I stole from you when I
was in your service. I hope it is not too late to ask your

29

forgiveness. We are both getting on now. Yours sincerely, May Prosser." No address was given.

"Isn't that peculiar?" my grandmother asked me. She read the note again and examined the trimmers. "May Prosser. I'd forgotten all about her. She left me years ago, before you were born." She rubbed the scrolled silverwork with a finger. "What a funny thing to do. I knew she'd stolen them, of course. Only one didn't like to say without proof. What can she be up to, giving them back now? Perhaps she's gone gaga."

"Gaga," I echoed, with a giggle.

My grandmother shrugged, and laid the trimmers aside. But as the hours went by, it became clear that the episode had unsettled her.

We passed the time, as was our routine on these visits, in her cluttered, overheated drawing room. She would lie on a chaise longue sipping cassis and scrutinizing the fashion pages in women's magazines. She had worked for such magazines in her day, and still counted herself an assiduous student of style. Her cheeks were always heavily rouged, and her lips were pearly pink. Pomanders, potpourri, and lavender bags filled the warm room with sweet dry odors, and such dust as I ever encountered while I idled on the floor was always scented with that same sweetness.

She loved jewelry, as did I. She wore quantities of it even though she rarely saw anybody, and she had books on the subject, filled with glossy pictures which I pored over each time I came to the flat. Sometimes she would let me open her jewelry box and spill its contents onto the carpet. Coral and lapis lazuli; pearls, jade, a ring made of gold that swirled like a turban, stripes of sapphire, florets of emerald and diamond, charm bracelets dangling silver animals with watch jewels for eyes, a great brooch of aquamarine . . . I could lose myself in rapture for hours over the contents of that box. "You ought to have been a girl"—my grandmother would laugh, then reach for her cassis, and sigh.

Sometimes, too, she would read to me. Our favorite tale was of the old Russian soldier who frightened death away by squeezing blood from a stone, only the stone was a beetroot. I liked the story for its cunning; she, I suppose, for its conclusion. I think she would have piled her kitchen high with beetroots had her sanity ever so much as wavered.

We passed much of the time in silence, absorbed in our own activities; comfortably aware of each other's presence, but feeling no obligation to speak.

However, on this day, the day of May Prosser's parcel, my grandmother became increasingly restless and talkative. From time to time she lowered her magazine, frowned, and observed how *very* peculiar, or strange, or odd it was of that woman to do what she had done. "A horrid little woman she was too," my grandmother said. "What can she want with me, I wonder?"

Then by degrees her attention turned from May Prosser to the candle-trimmers themselves.

"They belonged to *my* grandmother. When I was your age . . ." A stream of reminiscence began then to pour from her. The parcel had prized open a fissure in her, and her early life welled through. She talked and talked, quite oblivious of me, and was still talking when the nurse arrived to administer her drugs and help her bathe.

The following morning a registered letter arrived with May Prosser's writing on it. My grandmother looked at it with distaste. "You can open it," she said.

There was a banker's draft inside, for two and a half thousand pounds.

"Dear Mrs. Cranbourne," read the accompanying note. "Please accept this money in payment for the vase I broke and denied breaking. You knew I broke it but were kind enough not to make trouble for me. I don't know how much it was worth, you said thousands. I hope this is enough, it is all I have. Please do not think too ill of me. Yours sincerely, May Prosser."

"Oh," said my grandmother, "how dreadful." She looked forlornly at the draft. "How dreadful. She's sent me her life savings. She must be going senile. What shall we do?"

I looked up from my cereal uncertain what to say. For my part, I could see no problem. I had just begun to make the connection between money and happiness. I periodically made myself miserable wondering how someone so feeble as I felt myself to be could ever make enough money to be happy. Through sheer force of anxiety I had established a custom among my relatives, that they should tip me handsomely whenever I met them. I hoarded pennies, and felt it my sacred duty to appropriate any untended loose change I found in the households where my parents deposited me on their frequent travels abroad. I wanted to tell my grandmother that I would gladly take the money from May Prosser myself, if she felt unable to accept it. I had enough delicacy, however, to realize that now was not the moment to do so.

She looked so weary and troubled, there in her veils of

gauze, her eyelashes not yet on, her sparse wisps of red-
dish hair spirited into a frail dome over her scalp.

"What could I possibly want with her money? She
must be mad. The vase was insured anyway. We were
hoping somebody would break it. Such a horrible thing.
A relation of your grandfather's gave it to us as a wedding
present. It was a piece of expensive antique tourist junk
from Germany. A great big glass goblet with enameled
views of Bavarian castles all over it. Quite the ugliest
thing I ever owned."

We went slowly into the drawing room, her arm on
my shoulder, rose-scented talc swirling invisibly about
the folds and tucks of her gauzy nightgown.

"I shall dress after lunch," she said. She lay on her
chaise longue and reached for a magazine. I could see
the wrinkled flesh sagging from her arm as she stretched
it toward the pile. The blotches on her skin were big and
far apart, like the first raindrops on a pavement. I poured
out her glass of cassis. She gazed at the furred and jew-
eled models.

"I had a coat with a collar like that," she might say, or
"Those hats were fashionable in my day."

I took a pack of the brand-new playing cards of which
she had an endless supply, and spread them on the floor
for a game of Pelmanism against myself. Net curtains
made an area of milky light behind her. The deep red
bloom of an amaryllis on the television testified to the
tropical conditions of the room.

"She knows I don't need her money," my grandmother murmured. "Why does she send me these
things?" Then, as I matched two queens and proceeded
to redeem pair after pair from the spawn of cards on the
floor, she said, "Your grandfather was just like you. He

never forgot a thing. I, on the other hand, was always too muddled and light-headed to remember very much at all."

But now, as she lay sipping her cassis and watching my little feats of memory, her own memory began to belie those words. At first she picked randomly at her married life, much as I had done at my jumble of cards, mismatching people and incidents, dates and events, until gradually the episodes fell into place, and started to resurface in her mind with something approaching clarity.

"We visited Europe's capitals for our honeymoon. It took us almost a year."

She recalled the doorman's braided piping at a Viennese hotel, heat rash in Rome, how her husband was mistaken for the Grand Duke of Luxembourg in a lobby in Baden-Baden, an itinerant jeweler in Amsterdam tipping onto the embroidered cloth of their restaurant table a chamois pouch full of unset amethyst and tiger's eye, red champagne in Prague, triplets in maroon cloche caps tipsy in the enclosure at Chantilly. . . . She lay back sipping her cassis, remembering these things and the later years. She was not addressing me. The words streamed from her lips as if autonomous, and she, sallow beneath her rouge, seemed at once oblivious of and enrapt in them, like an exhausted medium transmitting a dead soul's testament.

My grandmother talked incessantly, the memories soon flowing too fast for her mind to separate them, so that the past became populated with strange hybrid events comprising such occasions as my mother's birth, my aunt's fiancé dying of shrapnel wounds, and a series of picnic breakfasts one summer on the South Downs. I could not follow her, and she, too, seemed estranged

from her own loquaciousness. By lunchtime her forehead was moist enough to reflect the milky light of the
netted window.

"I am overexciting myself," she said. "Here—" I
helped her to her feet, and we walked unsteadily to the
dining room. "I haven't thought about these things for
years," she told me as she served the veal and asparagus,
prepared by May Prosser's successor. "I don't think it is
very healthy to dwell on one's past. Do you?"

And to distract herself from it, she switched on the
television after lunch. She liked to watch the races, and
was giving me a taste of them too, by encouraging me to
gamble. She would hand me a pound to bet with—I
invariably chose the outsider with the longest odds. I
would take the pound down to the hall porter and ask
him to place my bet for me at the bookmaker. The porter
was inclined to pocket the money himself if he thought
the horse had absolutely no chance. We could see from
the window whether or not he went to place my bet, and
long ago we had discovered the added amusement of
gambling with each other on his capriciousness.

"I bet he doesn't go," I said to my grandmother, handing her a half crown which she was to return doubled if
I was proved correct.

I was, and anyway the horse fell at the first fence, as it
almost invariably did. It pleased my grandmother immensely to benefit both myself and the porter in this
way. She was a gracious giver; it flustered her to receive.

We allowed the television to divert us for the rest of
the day. My grandmother had personal feelings toward
the presenters and compères. She was of a generation
that experienced them as real people, not the corpora-
tive chimeras we now know them to be. She adored the
new breed of camp comedians taking over the shows.

"*Terribly* funny," she would say with a guilty smile, as if apologizing to someone who disapproved; or else, "He *does* make me laugh." To be made to laugh was, for her, the principal reason for having a television. She watched, figuratively speaking, with her ribs exposed, willing the performer to tickle them. The news bored her, quiz programs she disliked, though her real contempt was reserved for the soap operas, which left life as dreary as it was. "Why on earth do people want to watch these programs?" she would ask if we accidentally alighted on one in our quest for amusement.

By nighttime, when the nurse arrived, it seemed the morning's disturbance had been quite forgotten. And when nothing arrived in the post with the following breakfast, it seemed also that the remainder of my visit was going to pass in its customary tranquillity.

"Perhaps we might have tea at Fortnum's this afternoon," said my grandmother as she finished her last piece of toast.

But shortly after breakfast the doorbell rang, and there was the porter, a cigarette in one hand and a vast bouquet of roses in the other.

My grandmother caught her breath as I brought them into the drawing room.

"Dear Mrs. Cranbourne," the note with them read. "I am sorry to disturb you yet again, but I have just remembered one last thing. Some roses once arrived for you from a man called Geoffrey Isaacs. You had gone out, having lost your temper with me for no good reason. I took the roses myself out of spite. Please forgive. I hope I did no damage by my wickedness. God bless you. Yours sincerely, May Prosser."

My grandmother's face slackened into a look of haggard helplessness.

"Geoffrey Isaacs," she said quietly. She started to tug at the cellophane wrapper covering the roses, but soon gave up and laid them on the window ledge beside her. The roses were a lush velvety crimson. The wrapper glazed them, and they were wet too, big dewy beads of condensation dripping onto the furled red petals and dark green leaves from the inside of the cellophane.

We were quiet again that morning, but it was not a calm quiet. We lay as if we had eaten excessively and any activity beyond breathing was uncomfortable. We were superenriched—I have had that sensation since; it is as if your blood has been exchanged for some sweet creamy substance that swells in your veins until you feel over-ripe, overladen, and all you want to do is unburden yourself of everything that clots up your life. It can herald a severe depression, or a nosebleed, or a bout of insatiable sexual desire. It is pleasure taken to an unbearable extreme; a refined torment, only for those among whom superabundance is an occupational hazard. We lay still in that hot room; we were like Keats's bees in their overbrimmed, clammy cells.

Unanimated, my grandmother's face looked glum and old. Occasionally she sipped thoughtfully at her cassis and murmured to herself. "She oughtn't to have taken them," I heard her say, and "She oughtn't to have returned them," and once or twice, "Geoffrey Isaacs, well I never."

She looked drowsy on her chaise longue, and disheveled. She sighed. Neglected by her, I too became anxious and disconsolate. I was yearning to be older; to be able to control things. I had brought out my bubble-blowing kit to entertain myself that morning. I can remember dipping the plastic hoop into the soapy liquid, and then feeling incapable of breathing life into the taut, translucent membrane. Instead I watched its oil-bright colors swirl and dilate as if they were about to resolve themselves into some dazzling, tremulous sesame, never doing so before it burst.

I brought my grandmother's lunch in on a tray, but she laid it aside after staring at it miserably for a few moments. "I don't think I'll manage Fortnum's this afternoon," she said. Then, remembering her duties as my hostess, she added, "But shall we watch the races instead?"

I selected an outsider running at a hundred or so to one. She gave me a pound. I took the lift down to the mirrored hall and gave the money to the porter.

"I bet he will go today," I said, handing my grandmother one of the half crowns she had paid me the day before.

"Very well, dear."

I watched out the window, and sure enough the porter presently ambled out of the building, cigarette in one hand, my pound note in the other. I was aching; full of indefinable needs. Too much was passing through me, but I craved for more. I had to help myself to my half crowns from my grandmother's handbag, she feeling too listless to search for the coins herself. I opened the stiff, shiny bag, fingered through its freight of lipstick, tissues, powder compacts, credit cards, mirrors, and receipts, opened the soft leather purse and, thinking it would assuage my desire, took all the silver it contained, and the copper too.

We watched the race—I with my habitual excitement, she with a fearfulness that turned, as did my excitement, to a kind of nausea as we realized my outsider was going to win.

"Well, there you are," my grandmother said when it was over. "We've won a race."

We waited for the porter to arrive, avoiding each other's eyes, as if we had been caught at something shameful.

The bell rang. The porter stood there in a cloud of smoke, chuckling and twinkling, thrilled to be a bringer of such good tidings. he strode past me into the flat, holding our winnings in a carrier bag.

"You've done it," he bellowed. "I never thought the day would come. My congratulations to you, Mrs. Cranbourne, and to you, sir."

We wanted him to leave the bag and go, but he was waiting for us to rejoice with him. "Everyone's winning today," he said. "They ran out of notes. Here—" He reached into the bag and tossed me a dozen plastic envelopes full of coins. Some of the envelopes burst open with a clink as they hit the floor. The rest of the money was in notes, which he handed solicitously to my grandmother. We thanked him, but he wouldn't go. He stayed there grinning and puffing, as if he expected us to tip him, or at least count the money with him. Then he caught sight of my bubble-blowing kit.

"Look," he said to me, "I'll show you a trick." He dipped the hoop into the liquid, and inhaled deeply on his cigarette. He thought he was so cheerful, but at that moment he was hateful to us. Slowly and carefully he blew smoke into the drumhead of soap. We looked on silently as three big smoked-filled bubbles billowed out and drifted heavily toward the window. Daylight showed the smoke swirling inside the bubbles. It was the color of jaundiced porcelain. The heaviest bubble fell back toward my grandmother. She closed her eyes as it approached. It burst on her gemmed knuckle, releasing a gout of smoke that dispersed about the notes she was holding.

He blew a stream of smaller ones, which fell like silent bombs on the floor about me. We could not bring ourselves to applaud him, and waited silently for him to make his exit.

"Well," he said, "that's it. That's my trick. I'll be off then, shall I?" We made no effort to delay him.

Left to ourselves, we neither spoke nor barely stirred. My grandmother's eyelids drooped and she fell asleep. I tipped out the coins from all the plastic envelopes, and played with them. I counted them, I arranged them in big concentric rings, I stacked them into crooked columns that tottered precariously and crashed to the ground, I filled my mouth with them and spilled them out like a human fruit machine; I built them into mounds and swam my hands through them.

It was not until much later that it occurred to me that the notes, too, were mine to play with. The sky had darkened and the room was gray. I whispered, "Granny, can I have my money?" She made no response. I knew I should have let her be, but I could not help myself. I crept up to her. She was holding the notes in the air below the window ledge. The dark little rubies sparkled secretively from her knuckle. I reached my hand toward the fanning wad of notes clasped in her fingers. I pulled gently at the money but it refused to slip from her grasp. I was perplexed; I thought perhaps she was teasing me, or that she had decided not to let me keep the winnings after all. A tiny sensation of panic passed through me. I tugged sharply at the notes. They came away immediately, and as my hand shot upward it struck the bouquet of roses lying over the window ledge. Condensation had gathered in a dipped corner of the cellophane. As I struck it, the water slithered out of the hole in the corner and splashed down onto my grandmother's face. She did not flinch. The water broke into little quicksilver drops, which trickled over her powdered skin.

By the time the nurse came, it had collected at the scoop of her throat. It glinted there like a colossal jewel.

The Siege

M ARIETTA WAS WOKEN one night by a rumbling sound in the wall beside her bed. She switched on her lamp and opened the door to the dumbwaiter, which she used as a clothes cupboard. Her clothes lay neatly folded on the two shelves, as she had left them. But resting on a pile of shirts on the lower shelf was a piece of white cartridge paper. The address of the house was embossed in smart black print at the top, and below this was a large question mark painstakingly executed in turquoise ink:

$$?$$

She had no word, in English or her own language, for a dumbwaiter, and she had never considered what the original function of her clothes cupboard might have been. But it was a matter of seconds before she realized that it was in fact a small lift connecting her basement flat with the house upstairs. There was only one person living up there: Mr. Kinsky.

Marietta cleaned and ironed for Mr. Kinsky, in exchange for accommodation in his basement. It was a convenient arrangement, enabling her to study, while supporting herself frugally, but adequately, with a weekend job supervising a launderette.

She turned over the piece of paper. There was nothing there. A faintly disturbing thought occurred to her: she examined her shirts and blouses, bras and knickers, for signs of interference. Nothing seemed to be amiss. This did not greatly surprise her: she had judged Mr. Kinsky to be an eccentric, overbred product of European capitalism, but not a dangerous pervert. He had treated her with impeccable courtesy since her move here over a year ago. If anything, he was a little shy of her.

She resolved not to jeopardize her position by making a fuss. Whatever hopes and desires were encoded in that scroll of turquoise ink—and it was not difficult to guess —it seemed a harmless enough way of expressing them. She would say nothing; Mr. Kinsky would understand, and that would be that.

She threw the piece of paper away, closed the cupboard door, and went back to sleep.

She had lectures and classes the next day, and did not see Mr. Kinsky. But that night she was woken again by the rumbling of the dumbwaiter. This time it served her an orchid. Orange freckled with mauve, blue flames running along the center of each fluted petal. Lying there naked and unadorned, curved and contorted into itself, it looked like the embodiment of an indecent suggestion. Somewhat reluctantly, she picked it up. It was cool to the touch, sprung firmly upon its involutions. She couldn't quite bring herself to throw away something so fresh and brilliant, so she stuck it unceremoniously in the chipped mug of water by her bed.

She thought uneasily of Mr. Kinsky. Was he listening at his end of the shaft, trying to decipher a response from the sound of her movements? Foreseeing that this idea would only worry her into a sleepless night, she shrugged it off and climbed back into bed resolved, as before, to say nothing.

She was doing Mr. Kinsky's ironing in the small utility

room at the top of the house the following afternoon,
when she heard his tread on the staircase.

The door was open, and she could see him above as
he climbed the stairs. He was a very large man with a
slow, soft way of moving. His black hair was silvering but
still curly, and always unkempt. He wore a baggy black
suit, a white shirt buttoned at the collar, but no tie. His
broad face was almost entirely unmarked by care or suf-
fering, which gave it a serene handsomeness.

He did, however, look worried when he caught sight
of Marietta at the top of the stairs. She smiled at him
and said hello, in a perfectly nonchalant way.

"Ah . . ." he said, coming to a standstill in the doorway. He paused there, while she aligned the legs of a pair
of pajama bottoms and folded them up. He cleared his
throat, and waggled his fingers as if trying to conjure
more words from the air. None came, but still he lingered, making tortured expressions on his face, with an
unselfconsciousness that suggested he had little idea
how very imposing his presence was.

Marietta spread out a shirt on the ironing board and
pulled a trigger on the iron. Steam rose in a puff that
clouded out her hand. Mr. Kinsky stopped fidgeting and
stared at the phenomenon as if he had never seen anything so odd in his life. Presently he sighed, and padded
off next door, to his music room.

Marietta smiled to herself as she heard the scales peal
out from the grand piano. She had seldom managed to
discourage a suitor with such ease. The key of the scales
shifted up semitone by semitone, a steady spiraling ascent through the octave. The upward movement was
exhilarating, and Marietta listened to it happily, confident that Mr. Kinsky's affections were back where they
belonged: with his Steinway.

That night the rumbling came again. Marietta opened her eyes, more startled on this occasion than she had been before, and for the first time fractionally afraid. She lay quite still in the darkness, listening, but the house was absolutely silent. She could see the cupboard handle gleaming in the faint light that seeped through the curtain from a street lamp. She sat up slowly and stretched her hand toward it. She opened the door as quietly as she could.

A ring lay cushioned in the pile of shirts. She held it up to the window, twisting it in the light. Dark jewels glittered; a sodium burnish slid about the gold. It was heavy, and blood-warm from a hand's prolonged grasp. She felt suddenly vulnerable in her nakedness, as if there were a hundred eyes glinting in the shadows of her room. She placed the ring beside the orchid and pulled the blankets tightly about her body.

The ring was slippery in her hands, as she climbed the stairs to return it the following day. Big chords and rippling arpeggios rained down through the house from the music room. Mr. Kinsky had a taste for the rhapsodical to which Marietta, recognizing it as the luxurious rhetoric of the haute bourgeoisie spirit, was more or less indifferent. She only liked it when he toiled through his scales: something in the drudgery made her uncloak her sensibility, and listen.

She was nervous about the confrontation that awaited her. Life at Mr. Kinsky's had been simple and carefree. Now she suspected her luck was about to run out. It was an object lesson in the treacherous magnanimity of the powerful.

He continued playing, quite unaware of her as she

hovered in the doorway of the music room, clutching the ring in her hand.

The grand piano was positioned against a huge, gilt-framed mirror. Mr. Kinsky and his reflection conferred closely over an operation in the bass regions, then parted company for the upper extremities of their respective keyboards. The instrument itself, its lid propped open for maximum resonance, was doubled into a gigantic butterfly.

When finally Mr. Kinsky registered her presence, he stopped mid-cadenza and blushed, quite unashamedly. Can a blush be executed unashamedly? Yes, in that Mr. Kinsky appeared entirely unconscious of it: the blood came flooding into his cheeks, but he looked Marietta in the eye as if nothing were out of the ordinary, nothing at all.

"Ah . . . hello," he said.

Marietta walked briskly across the cork-tiled floor and placed the ring on a stack of yellow Schirmer's Library scores piled at the front of the piano.

"This is *yours*, I think?"

He looked impassively at the ring—a big oval emerald garnished with diamonds and gold filigree. His look was so inscrutable that for a moment Marietta wondered whether he was going to disclaim it.

"My aunt's," he said at last. He looked down at the keyboard and pressed a white note with a long, powerful-looking forefinger, so gently that although the leverage was visibly transmitted to the felt-covered hammer beneath the exposed strings, no sound was produced.

Marietta stood in the opulent curve of the instrument, waiting.

She knew that Mr. Kinsky had been brought up in this house by his aunt, a sparky-looking woman whose resplendent portrait hung in the dining room. She had wanted him to be a concert pianist. She drowned in a yachting accident when Mr. Kinsky was nineteen. *I found I couldn't perform after that*, Mr. Kinsky had said, *but then again she left me the house and enough money . . .*

"I was rather hoping you'd hang on to it, you know . . ." he said finally.

"Why?"

He stood up and lumbered over to the room's balcony window. Facing out of it, he began a long, meandering confession of love.

His shadow trailed out from his heels across the cork tiles. The floor surfaces in this house! Black and white checkered doorsteps, herringbone wood in the hall, cold granite flagstones in the kitchen, rush matting, goat-skins, Friesian cowhides clouded symmetrically like Rorschach blots, deep pile, junkers, Persian rugs so lustrous still that filaments of precious metal must have been twisted into the weave . . . It was dizzying to think that the man who trod them carried in his mind an image of her which, if she caught his drift correctly, he had been worshipping in secret and with mounting fervor from the first week of her installment in his basement.

He turned to her. "I do love you, though, Marietta. I absolutely"—he waggled his fingers in desperation—"love you. I'm in love." He faced her with a trancelike stare, relishing the word as if it were some exquisite delicacy he had never tasted before—"I love you."

She felt mildly intrigued by the emotions of this peculiar man, but could not in any way connect them with herself.

He looked so innocent, and clownish, buttoned up

like a schoolboy waiting for mother to tie his tie and comb his straggling curls. . . .

But then she happened to glance down at the piano top, and noticed a piece of manuscript paper with a bass and treble clef immaculately scrolled in turquoise ink at each stave, and back with a jolt came the question mark, the orchid, the ring, the dumbwaiter's rumbling underscore to Mr. Kinsky's quaint declaration. . . . She decided it was time to retreat.

"I think I should go." She made for the door.

Mr. Kinsky strode across the room to intercept her. He caught her wrists.

"Would you like to marry me?"

She could feel the beat of his heart pulsing through his big hands, and she could smell him too, a sweet rich tang.

"I couldn't possibly marry you!" She said it with a laugh that came out as a shrill, nervous giggle.

He was serious, he said; he had never had such feelings before. Marietta was determined not to let indignation, or embarrassment, or fear get the better of her, but she could feel herself shaking in his grasp.

He pulled her close to him and asked if she believed he was serious. Yes. Did she love him? No, please let me go. . . . Was there anything he could do to make her love him? No, please . . . Anything at all, was she sure? Let go of me!

"*Anything*, Marietta . . ."

She wrenched herself free. A furious glare burst behind her eyes, and before she could stop herself she shouted at him. In doing so, she revealed a secret she had been guarding since her arrival in London: "Get my husband out of jail!"

A pause.

"Your husband." Mr. Kinsky sat down on the piano stool. "I didn't realize you had a husband."

Marietta stepped back, and watched him with the nervously satisfied eye of someone who has dislodged a small, critically placed stone, and set off an avalanche.

"May I ask what he is doing in jail?"

She emptied the bucket of water down the front steps. Steaming suds cascaded over the black and white checkered stone and slithered out onto the pavement, darkening it. She picked up the mop and began to clean, leaving the front door open. Pale sunlight glistened on the bubbles of soap. Scales poured down from the music room, a torrent of sound streaming out of the door and down into the street.

There had been a shift in the atmosphere of the house. It was like the modulation from major to minor in Mr. Kinsky's scales, which always gave Marietta a feeling of foreboding, a premonitory tingle, when she heard it. The incident in the music room had pitched them into a somber, melancholic key. To be sure, the dumbwaiter no longer rumbled in the night, and she had not been asked to leave. Nevertheless, she and Mr. Kinsky were no longer comfortable with each other. For weeks now, Mr. Kinsky had been conspicuously avoiding her when she came upstairs to his part of the house. She didn't mind this, but it coincided with a growing anxiousness on her part. She had begun to wake up in the mornings feeling worried and unrested. Certain questions about her life, which she had succeeded in shelving since her arrival in England, were now stirring again, clamoring for an answer. These questions concerned her husband, from whom she had not heard since his incarceration in the military barracks of her country's capital city four years ago. She had no idea whether she would see him again, or whether he was even alive.

She was a conscientious worker. The steps were dazzling by the time she had finished them. She went indoors and set to work on the shelves and niches in Mr. Kinsky's drawing room.

She was deep in thought as she moved about the room. Four years and an ocean away from a husband who might or might not be alive, she had remained wedded to the idea of him. It was surprisingly easy to consecrate oneself to such a mystery, like falling asleep in snow. It formed a backdrop to her life in London that made this life less purposeless than it might have been otherwise, though it did so only because she took pains not to examine it too closely. But since she had revealed its existence to Mr. Kinsky, the mystery had begun to appear once more in the foreground of her thoughts, and when it did it was like one of those vast unanswerable metaphysical questions that creep up and stun you into panic at the sheer unlikeliness of you being alive, here, now.

There was one shelf which Mr. Kinsky had asked her to take particular care over. It contained a number of objects that were without exception, he said, quite priceless. Her hands were long accustomed to the shape and weight of them all, so that she could give each one its due care without needing to break out of her reverie. Scarcely seeing what she was doing, she steadied and dusted a winged gray bust of Mercury, an art nouveau vase fashioned from the attenuated bodies of a man and woman entwined, a frail and worn fragment of an ancient ivory horse. . . . Absently she put out her hand to

grasp the little statuette of shepherds and nymphs that
had always stood next in line. She found herself grasping
at air. The statuette was gone.

The absence stalled her for a moment, but she gave it
no further thought.

Until a week later, when she noticed that a framed
original manuscript, signed by its composer, was missing
from the upstairs landing. She wasn't inquisitive by nature, but her curiosity was aroused, and she kept her
eyes open for other disappearances.

She came upon four square patches of paler paint on
the wall in one of the spare rooms; memorials to a row
of watercolors depicting scenes from Kiev, one for each
season. A circular imprint on top of a corner cupboard
was all that remained of a large Oriental vase. And
hadn't there been a little clutch of enameled lockets in
that wicker basket?

She had never been greatly interested in Mr. Kinsky's
affairs. She assumed he lacked for nothing. He lived off
a private income, from which she deduced he had
money invested in countries such as her own, where
governments could be relied upon to keep wages negli-
gible, and profits correspondingly enormous. This made
him reprehensible, though in too passive a way for her
to be able to maintain an individual grudge against him.
She merely hoped, and believed, that his breed would
one day vanish from the face of the earth.

But the disappearance of these objects conferred an
air of mystery upon him. Was he simply bored with them
or did he need money? If the latter, then . . . It was good
to be able to think about someone not connected with
her own affairs. Mr. Kinsky was out at the moment. The
only sound was of the spring wind rattling windows in
the big, airy rooms. She began to search the house. An

ornamental silver bowl was missing from the dining room table. Was he in some sort of trouble? She went into his study. Where was the chair with lion paws at its feet, a gilt lion head carved at the front of each armrest? What was going on?

She began to feel uncomfortable lingering in Mr. Kinsky's private study, so she turned to go, but as she left she glimpsed something in the wastepaper basket that made her stop in her tracks. It was an envelope, crumpled but with part of the stamp still showing. She picked it up and smoothed it out. It was addressed to Mr. Kinsky. The stamp, as she had suspected, was familiar to her, more than familiar. It bore the face of a man with a general's hat and a thick-jowled look of military displeasure. He was the president of her own country. She looked at him in wonder, and as she stood there thinking, her wonder turned to amazement, and finally to a kind of helpless awe as a suspicion of what Mr. Kinsky might be doing, or trying to do, assembled itself from the evidence in her hand and all around the house, and rose up within her, creeping under her skin, like a blush. . . .

Mr. Kinsky was learning a new piece. He started practicing it in the morning before Marietta went to her classes, and would still be at it when she returned in the afternoon. Day after day he played nothing but this piece.

It began with a childish melody, a simple nursery tune of no particular distinction. The tune was played again and again, but at each repetition a new element was added to the accompanying harmonies, deepening and darkening its resonance, so that it was gradually transformed from its bland cheerfulness into something haunting and disturbing, in the way that a child's toy might be if you were to see it in a series of successively gloomier backgrounds, beginning with a nursery and ending with a graveyard. Then when it had reached its graveyard phase, the tune was abandoned, and the piece burst into the most voluptuous, ecstatic progression of pounding bass notes and dazzling runs cascading down from higher and higher.

She heard the piece now as she sat at her desk by the window, trying to gain a foothold in the huge textbook that lay before her. Through sheer force of repetition, the music had begun to get the better of her customary immunity, and steal its way into her system. Here was the tune again—la da da *da*-de-da. . . . Here was that first hint of shadow in its harmony, then another, deeper, deeper . . . She stared out the window and watched the breeze winnowing white blossoms from an almond tree. Flurries of fallen petals were swirled up into ghostly tops and sent spinning across the street . . . Here was the tune in its twilight stage; she felt her body tensing up in expectation. . . . There! The first pounding volley as the piece exploded into rhapsody—bombs and shrapnel, starbursts of sound.

It was impossible to work. Like Mr. Kinsky's confession of love, the discovery of her president in the wastepaper basket had transformed the atmosphere around Marietta. She had begun to feel peculiarly sensitive, alert to every movement and disturbance. And there was a profusion of disturbances, of stirrings and awakenings. . . .

The house was steadily being denuded. Every time she went upstairs something else was missing, and each time she noticed it her heart gave a jump. She was in a state of mild but continuous trepidation. One by one the prize possessions had disappeared from their special shelf. Now only the gray bust of Mercury remained. Seeing him standing there alone, she had been struck for the first time by his beauty. He had clusters of curls under his winged helmet. His face had been sculpted with great delicacy—a trace of Olympian amusement on his lips, his cheeks cool and smooth to the touch. . . .

And yesterday an unsigned letter had arrived for her. *My dear Marietta, news of your husband: he is alive. He has been transferred from the barracks to an ordinary prison. I shall write again as soon as I know what is happening.*

Mr. Kinsky stumbled over a note, paused a moment, and returned to the beginning of the piece—la da da *da*-de-da. . . . How unnerving it was to be at the center of all this activity, but not its source. The powerlessness of her position made her feel by turns blissful and resentful. Several times she had been on the point of confronting Mr. Kinsky with her discovery, but to confess that she had guessed what he was doing would oblige her either to tell him he shouldn't, or else to acknowledge herself massively indebted to him. It was easier to pretend she knew nothing. Besides, Mr. Kinsky had become less communicative than ever. When he wasn't at his Steinway, he would be sitting in his unlit study, gazing into space with an air of broody preoccupation. She did not like to disturb him: she had begun to find his presence daunting, almost forbidding, as if with the disappearance of each possession, a commensurate space had been hollowed out in him and filled with shadow. He loomed large in her imagination.

She could not concentrate. She took her finger from the left-hand corner of the enormous book. The thin, silky pages bulged toward the center. Four or five of them slid in succession from the sprung sheaf and swung through the air in a lazy arc, settling gently on the other side.

It was raining. Thin drops crackled against the window. Water trickled in plaited sluices from the gutters. She shuddered. Her room felt sparse and constricting. She had an urge to move.

She went upstairs. Today was not one of her working days, but she could always find some task. For a while she wandered aimlessly over the rugs and mats, the wood floors and stone floors. . . . She opened the drawing room door to look at Mercury. When she saw the gap where he had stood she had to steady herself against the doorframe. Wind made rumbling sounds in the windows, playing them like kettledrums.

She climbed upstairs to the utility room. La da da *da*-de-da . . . Here it was again, at full volume now, percussive chimes so bright and loud the space about Marietta seemed to be occupied not by air but by sound. She set up the ironing board and switched on the iron. Above her, suspended from the ceiling, was a cradle of bars over which the two large white sheets of Mr. Kinsky's double bed were draped. She reached up and pulled one toward her, furling it in as it slid free of its bar. It smelled sweet and clean. Bunched against her breast, it was like a colossal almond flower. She laid it over the ironing board. It was satisfying to cleave the iron through the linen waves and see the smooth white wake stretch out behind. She moved her arm in time with the music. She was thinking of her husband, or trying to: it was difficult to focus her thoughts while the music was swirling about her. A long swelling crescendo brought it to a pitch where it no longer sounded like a single piano, but a whole orchestra. She glanced through the open door of the music room. There he sat, lost deep inside his broad bulk, pouring out music like some mythical hoof-struck spring. And as she returned to her thoughts, the sound became a stream flooding down through the house, bearing a flotilla of enameled lockets, silver bowls, watercolors, Persian carpets, statuettes, engravings, jewels, furniture. . . .

It was like a forcible initiation. Day by day the music inducted her further into its secret language of nostalgia and desire. She had always considered it the height of decadence to have one's emotions tickled and stroked and cosseted in this way, for the sake of nothing more than a series of fleeting sensations. But as she became increasingly attuned to the nuances of the piece, so it grew more difficult for her to recall with any conviction the context within which the pleasure it gave was corrupt. She observed herself succumbing to it with a certain mortified fascination.

She sat in the Blue Ocean Launderette. Her duties here were minimal—dispensing change, tending the occasional service wash, sweeping the floor, closing up.

The machines were like a row of submarine portholes, looking onto a sea swirling with bright clothing. The melody was playing in her head—la da da *da*-de-da. She looked absently through the portholes. . . . Another letter had arrived that morning: *My dear Marietta, your husband has been granted a trial.* . . .

As she stared at the machines she tried to imagine what it would be like to start living again with a man she had not seen for four years. But she found herself instead remembering Mr. Kinsky's confession of love: the turquoise question mark, the orchid, the ring . . . turning from the balcony—*I do love you though, Marietta. I absolutely* . . . waggling his fingers, grimacing, lumbering across the room—*Would you like to marry me?* Grasping her wrists—*Anything at all . . . Anything, Marietta* . . . Clothes tumbled round and round. Lacy white suds splashed against the glass and slid away. Glissando runs echoed in her memory. . . . She had a sudden desire to be back in the doorway of the music room, watching Mr. Kinsky play. She closed her eyes. She realized that she could hardly wait to lock up and go home. A strange feeling ran through her: it had in it both exultation and dread.

It was still light when she locked up. It had been raining, but now a chink of blue had opened up in the clouds, and the sun was shining through, reflecting in gutters and puddles. She walked briskly along the street. Everything looked very clean and shiny. The buses seemed a brighter red, the taxis a glossier black. There was a bracing, astringent smell, like the smell of a new leaf crushed between two fingers. She felt almost light-headed among the jostling pedestrians, who were afflicted by a rare and visible exuberance of spirits. A chef stood in the doorway of his restaurant, sharpening a knife and looking critically at the sun. He was dressed in spotless white, a white scarf knotted at the side of his neck, and a lopsided hat. Every time he brought the blade down against the honing bar, it came out of the shadow of the doorway and flashed brilliantly in the sun, as if repeatedly puncturing a vein flowing with light. He smiled at Marietta as she passed, and without thinking she smiled back. Pigeons were strutting about, surveying the pavement cracks for the rainfall's harvest of worms. They cocked their heads and swelled their necks in jerky spasms; and when a puffed-up throat twisted in the light, the modest gloss of green and violet made Marietta think of a black-and-white photograph puffing and straining to be color, and she giggled to herself at the thought. She had an urge to run. How peculiar this feeling was—a strange, aching elation. She turned into her road. The almond trees were sparkling with waterdrops. They had been stripped by the wind of all but a few tight white bunches of blossom that clung like crowns of fleece to the shiny black twigs. The trees gleamed in their mantles of water like moss in agate.

Something seemed to be happening at the house. She could see people standing on the pavement outside. She quickened her pace. There was a small crane that had been hidden by the angle of the building. She began to run. She could hear the deep rumble of the crane's motor, and the squeak of revolving pulleys. She arrived in time to see the grand piano, trussed in thick ropes, rise up from the music room's balcony window, swing slowly away from the house, and descend majestically to the pavement, where a removal lorry awaited it.

The silence in the house was terrible. It resonated in the big, empty rooms.

Marietta sat at her desk in a daze. She could no longer even pretend to work. From time to time she heard the music in her head—la da da *da*-de-da—twitching like a phantom limb, and when she heard it, she was filled once more with that strange, dreadful exultation, only now the discomfort of the feeling far outweighed the pleasure.

She had been once into the music room: where the mirror had formerly doubled the piano, it now doubled its absence, and the bareness of the place made her ache. She found herself waggling her fingers as Mr. Kinsky had done when searching for words to express his feelings for her.

The next letter to arrive was from her husband himself; a short note telling her that he was free, and that he would be arriving in England in a fortnight, five days of which had elapsed since the letter was posted. No need to meet him at the airport.

It wasn't unexpected; all the same, Marietta was surprised at her lack of reaction. It might have been a gas bill, for all the effect it had on her. She wondered if this was the numbness people are supposed to experience when they first go into shock. If so, what would she feel when it wore off?

It occurred to her that she ought to inform Mr. Kinsky. She went upstairs, feeling as apprehensive as she had been months earlier, when she had climbed up to return his ring. She was struck by the peculiar symmetry of the two occasions—every aspect was inverted: anger had turned into a kind of furtive gratitude, fear into wonder, unheard music into this tumultuous silence.

He was lying on a sofa in the drawing room. It was a long sofa, but he was even longer; his legs stuck out over the armrest. She could see a section of very white shin between the end of his puckered trousers and the beginning of his socks. He wasn't doing anything. He looked calm and self-possessed.

"Hello, my dear." He used the endearment with the authority of someone who has acquired a right to it precisely by virtue of his grace in defeat as a prospective lover.

"I just wanted to ask you if . . ." She could hear her voice wobbling like a timid child's. "I just wanted to ask you if it was all right for my husband to move into the flat. He's been released." She looked down at the bare floor. She could sense him staring at her. She peeped up; he was. It was a complex, eloquent stare. It invited her to divulge more about this turn of events; it forgave her if she chose not to.

"What marvelous news. You must be very happy." He didn't sound the least bit surprised.

"Yes," she said, "I just heard. He'll be here in a week, just over a week."

"That's frightfully exciting."

"Yes." The space in the room seemed taut, contracted: a bubble that the slightest slip would burst. She realized that this would probably be her last opportunity to acknowledge Mr. Kinsky's magnanimity. The charade of ignorance she was going through would otherwise soon harden into an established version of the truth that would be difficult ever to breach without awkwardness and embarrassment. An act of monumental generosity would simply evaporate from history if she did not speak now.

They looked at each other for a moment, both watching the opportunity go by. Then Mr. Kinsky said of course her husband could move in, and that he looked forward to meeting him. She gave him the faintest of smiles, and went back downstairs, her legs trembling, ever so slightly.

What had she been afraid of? That he would attempt to hold her to an ironic, rhetorical promise? She tried to make herself believe that this was the case. With that in mind, she reread her husband's letter, attempting to induce the rush of joy that had failed to materialize first time round. If she succeeded, then she would be able to attribute the feelings of elation that arose in her whenever she thought of Mr. Kinsky to his services in bringing back her husband; the feelings of dread to what he might ask in return.

She did not succeed. In fact, she felt her spirits beginning to sink. How appalling . . . She struggled. *He's free,* she told herself, *he's coming back to me.* . . . She pictured him walking through the door. The first kiss . . . would it be passionate? sexual? Would he want to make love before they spoke? Would she want to? Would the circumstances oblige her to? She hadn't slept with a man for four years. She imagined herself naked in his arms, his mouth at her breast, his hands sliding between her legs. Her heart burst into life, but it was not desire that beat there. It was panic; dread.

Thus it was that Marietta drifted into the realm of pure emotion. Her flat and the streets beyond were less real to her now than the shimmering landscape of feelings she found herself stranded in. She had never been anywhere so strange and treacherous. She had a clear objective: to persuade herself that she loved her husband, and that she did not love anybody else. She was perfectly sincere in her desire to do this. Her husband was a good and brave man for whom she had the utmost admiration and respect. Their marriage—an alliance of idealists against a common oppressor—had been exciting and happy. A certain anxiety was to be expected after an interval of four years. But this was much more than anxiety: this was cold sweats in the small hours when she thought of him in bed beside her; nausea at mealtimes when she considered the unending wifely devotion he was entitled to, and would certainly need after his ordeal; a sudden flushing out of all the strength from her limbs as she imagined the sheer saturation to which his presence would subject the little flat.

The closer the day came, the worse these symptoms grew. The harder she tried to overcome them, the more exhausted she became. She had never before experienced the full waywardness of feelings. It exasperated her that an invisible, intangible phenomenon like love, which could barely be said to exist at all, could not be brought to heel.

Love, desire, fear, revulsion . . . Feelings are like a physicist's massless particles, the hypothetical agencies by which the universe coheres and makes itself visible. These miraculous phenomena combine all-pervasiveness with absolute elusiveness, ceasing to exist when not in motion. Devoid of any intrinsic qualities, their secondary effects are nonetheless momentous and ineluctable. A particle of desire is as improbable as a photon or a graviton; its effects are as undeniable as light, or gravity.

In the middle of the night before her husband was due to arrive, Marietta awoke with jolt. Her hand was at her groin, and her groin was moist. She could hear, as an internal echo rather than an actual sound, a deep rumbling, as though she had just been woken by such a noise. She opened the door of the dumbwaiter. There was nothing there. In her groggy state this seemed wrong. She rummaged frantically through her clothes: nothing at all. She felt cheated out of something. Her dream had lurched her into wakefulness just as she had reached the pitch of arousal, and it was like being lurched into a void. She remembered lying on an odd-shaped bed. There was a radial of taut silky strands running through her body from her breast. A hand touched her nipple; squeezed it gently between finger and thumb. The strands tautened, transmitting a vibrant current of desire throughout her body. The owner of the finger and thumb was in shadow. The slightest movement of his hand sent a sweet shudder of pleasure through her. She peered into the shadow. A face loomed forward. That was when she imagined the rumbling sound, and woke up. Recalling this, she could not avoid also recalling whose face it was that had loomed toward her. She closed her eyes and buried her head in her pillow, trying to stifle both the recollection and the renewed pang of desire it brought with it.

Her capacity for self-deception, never great, was now all but exhausted. Nonetheless, as she got out of bed she told herself it was only to make herself a hot drink. And as she went, not to her kitchen, but to the stairway leading up to Mr. Kinsky's house, she told herself she merely wanted to sit for a while in his music room, alone. Even when she opened the door to Mr. Kinsky's bedroom and crept in, she half-believed that all she wanted to do was look at him as he slept.

He was fast asleep, breathing quietly and deeply. His massive body swelled and subsided beneath the pale blankets. The strands of silver in his black hair were just visible in the darkness. She felt tranquil looking at him; not in the least like an intruder. She slipped into the double bed beside him. The bed was warm from the heat of his body. She caught the soapy smell of his pajamas, which she had ironed only that morning. She put her hand on his waist, and leaned over to kiss him on the lips. His eyes opened.

"Marietta," he whispered.

"Sssh."

He lay still as she caressed him, as if afraid that the

slightest stir would make her vanish. She slid over his body, and she was astride him, sighing to herself. She grasped his wrists. The tighter she held them, the further away she was, tilting back her head, her shoulders, arcing her back like a bow, shuddering. Somewhere in her protracted orgasm he felt his own—a minor detail it seemed—drowned out by the high, inhuman cry that burst from her lips and echoed through the empty house long after she had fallen asleep at his side.

Shortly after daybreak they heard the squeal of a taxi's brakes outside the front steps. They held each other tightly in the short pause before Marietta's doorbell rang.

Escapes

STEVEN FARAH PICKED UP the photograph of his wife from his bedside table and slipped it between two cream shirts in the large mahogany wardrobe.

He checked his watch, then went out of the hotel to buy a bottle of wine from the vintners on the Avenue de Suffren. For three reasons he settled on the cheapest bottle: first, in case nothing should happen and the money be wasted (he would never consider drinking the bottle on his own); then in case something did happen, but at Lena's flat rather than at his hotel; and last, because if all went according to plan, the quality of the wine would be of little material importance.

Back at the hotel, he showered and began slowly to dress himself in front of the wardrobe's full-length mirror. The shutters were closed, and the only source of light was the dim lamp on the low bedside table. This threw flattering reflections across the contours of Steven's body, and gave a false richness to the grayish-brown pigment of his skin. He stood half naked, admiring himself for a moment; poised like this, his blackness seemed unvitiated by the streak of whiteness that he held responsible for everything he disliked about himself. In this light he could recreate in his mind the good-humored confidence and the sense of completeness that he imagined flavored the lives of his colleagues at the

71

institute. He tried to make his eyes twinkle the way Delmore Norton's had done when he told Steven about Lena. "Ring her up, man"—Steven repeated the words to his reflection, his eyes twinkling away—"check her out. She's a lovely girl. You'll have a good time." And he broke into a broad grin, which he suppressed, as he always did, when he was reminded that beneath his full, convincing lips nestled a brood of mean little Anglo-Saxon teeth.

He was a little nervous as he set out for the Métro. He forbade himself to check that his hundred-franc notes were still in the zippered section of his wallet—and checked twice before he reached the station. He wished he had not brought his fat volume of Joseph Campbell to read on the train—it stuck so visibly out of his pocket, and Lena might think he was trying to impress. He turned it upside down, but wouldn't that look too deliberate? How tiresome his little mind could be.

But his spirits rose now as he stepped from the Métro into the warm lilac evening. The thin sheet of cloud that enclosed the city was broken in the west, and split cones of sunlight made bullion out of glass and concrete office blocks. This phenomenon never failed to make Steven feel less ordinary than he was, though of course he realized the feeling was, in itself, the height of ordinariness.

He sat at an empty table outside the bar. Red trousers, she had said, blond hair, and a black jacket or beige cardigan, depending on the weather.

He stared hard at every passing blond, red-trousered or not, and one or two smiled faintly back at him before passing on. That made him feel immensely happy, and seemed auspicious. He checked his watch and his wallet, and chastised himself, but indulgently, making allowances for the circumstances, which were remarkably similar to those out of which he had lost his virginity to Gloria, who now lay muffled between the two cream shirts.

He still believed himself to be in love with Gloria—at least, he had had no fantasies about mourning her (sure sign, according to Delmore, of the passing of love)—but he had succeeded in arguing himself into a position of temporary heartlessness. He had made his decision; a man must lose two virginities before he can be regarded as fully initiated into modern society. First adultery is as essential as first love. There was no going back now. The firmness of the intention seemed a guarantee of its successful achievement, so that Steven had long thought of it as a *fait* lacking not will but merely circumstance to be *accompli*. And now that the conference on black culture had brought him to Paris on his own, and Delmore had put him onto his Dutch friend Lena, and he had spent all day feeding himself with desire until he felt almost poisoned with it, and the evening air was warm and sweet, and . . . and there scissoring into his vision was a pair of blood-red trousers.

Their blond, beige-cardiganed owner looked at, then past, Steven. But Steven stood up, rasping his green metal chair against the pavement, and thrust forward his hand, saying, "Lena?"

A fraction of a second's hesitant, appraising look, and then the clear Nordic face broke into a wide smile. "Hello, it's Steven, yes?" She took his hand and held it saying, "It's so lovely to meet you. I was so pleased when you rang. I'm always so *excited* to meet new people. Shall we stay here awhile? It's such a nice bar, don't you think? . . ."

And they were away. She, made voluble by coffee after coffee; he, sipping at topaz beers, putting in a judicious comment here, a wry smile there. His professorial persona had descended upon him, as it tended to do in times of uncertainty, but for the moment he felt succored rather than constricted by it, and he knew he would drink enough to shake it off when it became necessary to do so.

He felt in control, but *really* in control, and as his tongue danced through an anecdote about the white waiters at the conference banquet, he was thinking how astonishingly easy this business was after all, and how very enjoyable. She laughed generously at his story, and pressed him for more. She really was quite delightful; the tanned pink symmetry of her face, the pearl-sheened lips busily presenting him with yet more flattering images of himself, till he began to feel dizzy with self-esteem (those absurd suspicions he had had, that Delmore might have been setting him up with some kind of harridan as a practical joke!).

They wandered off along the crowded street in search of a Greek restaurant Lena knew. The air still smelled of fish from the day's market, and the pavements were strewn with discarded cabbage leaves and yellow cherries, and the occasional much-trampled pink rose or scarlet tulip. Steven wanted to make some bold gesture, like clasping Lena's hand, when she took his arm, and the contact made him want to rustle like a bird after preening. The perfect mauve coronets of a rhododendron pushing through some black railings seemed to be glowing, like Chinese lanterns in the dusk. Steven's patter evaporated, and Lena, too, appeared content to stroll on in silence.

They chose a linen-draped table outside the restaurant.

"I'm not so hungry," Lena said, relinquishing Steven's

arm. "I'll have just a salad. But you have a proper meal
—you're so thin! Have the *brochette de luxe*; it's good.
I'll enjoy watching you eat it!"

Steven drank to disinhibit himself. Professor Farah
dissolved in the thick white wine. A flower seller thrust
lemon-yellow roses at Steven—*"Pour la jolie fille."* He
waved her off, but how simple, he thought, and inexor-
able was this machinery coupling them.

Only now he must begin steering the conversation
from the impersonal toward the intimate. Perhaps he
could begin by conveying to her, suitably modified, what
Delmore had said about her and how true it was. But
no, there was something dangerously coarse and mer-
cantile there, and he forbade himself to explore that avenue.

But, "Delmore," he heard himself saying, "told me I
would be charmed by you, but I must say, I never expected someone quite so lovely as yourself."

Lena looked perplexed, then laughed faintly, then
looked sideways up at a tall, gaunt African wearing half
a dozen hide cowboy hats, who had come, heaven-sent,
to deflect the moment's tension by assailing them with
leather bags and hats and ivory bracelets. Steven could
hardly bear to look at the black radiance of the man's
face, the quizzical twinkle in his eye that seemed for an
instant to claim vestigial bonds but then turned leaden
again as Steven shook his head.

"Enough black culture for one day?" Lena said, her
irony not malicious but somehow still accusatory. Steven was excused from answering by the dry block of
lamb to which his jaws at that point were fully commit-
ted. He could feel sweat gathering at the back of his neck
in preparation for its oily descent along the groove of his
spine.

The thick, ill-chewed meat lay like ballast in his stomach. His mind, too, had lost its buoyancy, and he felt he was sinking.

"Where . . . where exactly do you live?" he asked, clutching at banality and regretting at once the uncalculated innuendo. Oh, but how he loathed that white maggot in him, always writhing with regret and anxiety, always squirming with fear, and abasing itself in a slavish desire to please and be well-liked. . . . He must destroy it, impale it with his willpower. What if there was an innuendo? Let it stand; be firm!

"I'll walk you home," he said, not having registered where home was.

"Oh, that's nice of you." She smiled sweetly and seemed genuinely pleased. "I love to walk in Paris. Only where I live it's not so safe for a girl to walk alone. Too many . . . nasty-looking people about."

Steven caught her clumsily avoided gaffe, and was pleased; it gave him a certain advantage.

"But there's no need to go immediately," he said.

"No, no. It's so lovely. . . . I could stay here talking all night."

And they were back on course again. Only now Steven took care to resist all temptation toward verbal strategies; he would be spontaneously physical, when the propitious moment came. He talked sternly about the aims of the conference, edging his mind into the man he had glimpsed in the mirror earlier on that evening. And just as he had been conscious of an illusory strength of physique then, so now he was conscious of a kind of bristling of psychic musculature, designed to convey a similar illusion of strength. He knew it was not an illusion he could maintain indefinitely.

Finally, they set off on the long march north toward

the Rue du Faubourg Poissonnière. No hand slipped into the crook of Steven's arm, but then if it had, that might have bound physical contact into the domain of the purely innocent, so Steven was not entirely dismayed.

He was about to remark on the extraordinarily stirring sense of vigor he felt emanating from the crowded street they were on—the Rue Saint-Denis—when he noticed, in the shape of a girl trussed in nets and leather, the probable explanation for this vigor.

He resumed his topic—the traumas of emancipation —his eyes chastely on the pavement before him, feigning indifference to the thickening shoals of mermaid-gladiators shimmering in the doorways. Until Lena interrupted him mid-flow and said, laughing, "So what do you think of the whores in this town?"

Despite the laughter, the question seemed to demand a correct answer, rather than merely an opinion. Steven wondered what the correct answer was, then said carefully, "Well, I'm attracted to them in an animal sort of way, but as a human being it pains me to see women being exploited like this. . . ."

Lena laughed again. "Oh, come on," she said, "you're lusting after them, and that's perfectly natural. Nobody's exploiting them. They're doing it out of choice, they make half a million francs a year like this." She tightened her beige cardigan about her waist, and Steven, uneasy with the subject, forced the conversation into a more neutral vein.

The moment was approaching. They had reached the end of the long, dark, silent street where Lena lived. Cobbles gleamed in the dim lamplight. A large bundle of sacking dumped on the railings of a ventilation shaft turned out to be two stupefied tramps.

"Lena . . ." Steven said.

"Yes?"

"You . . . haven't even told me what it is you do."

"Oh, it's much too boring. . . ."

At that moment, there was a scuffling of feet behind them. They turned around. Two men were running toward them. One of them, quite unmistakably, had a gun in his hand, and was chasing the other one, an Algerian. In two seconds, the Algerian had caught up with them, the gunman following close on his heels. "Come on—" shouted Lena, backing carefully away. Steven followed her, but the Algerian grabbed hold of the back of his jacket, sending a button flying from his blue shirt, and spun him around so that he formed a protective shield between himself and the gunman, whose black pistol was now pointed directly at Steven's exposed belly. In the same instant, Steven shot out an arm and grabbed hold of Lena, unintentionally impeding her retreat. But then, as he tore himself away from the Algerian, he made up for that by sweeping her with him twenty yards down the pavement while the two men scuttled off down a side street.

They walked on in silence for a moment. For Steven, that process of reconstruction one automatically applies to unusual incidents was delayed by a troubled awareness that he had secured the advantage of a handhold about Lena's waist, but in such a way as would make any exploitation of it seem the depths of ungentlemanliness. The arm twitched, then went slack and returned to his side, as if entirely self-responsible.

Lena was panting, and looked flushed. She put her hand to her heart and swallowed, and shook her straight blond hair.

"God, I'm trembling," she said. "That was a gun in his

hand, wasn't it? I feel quite shaken. . . ." And they began simultaneously describing to each other what had happened—excitedly reliving the danger of it, and the comedy too. "Did you see the button fly off my shirt? I felt like something in a cartoon!"

Then abruptly they had stopped, and Lena was fumbling in her back pocket for her night key.

"If you're quick," she said to Steven, "you might catch the last train from Barbès Rochechouart. It's just there at the end of the street." She found her key and inserted it into the lock. Steven looked dumbly at the serrations as they were swallowed up. Then he looked at Lena's candid face smiling at him and telling him how lovely it had been meeting him, and get in touch if ever . . . And he felt like a man who after hours of struggling to cajole sleep realizes he is wide awake, that he was wide awake even in those moments when he thought he was almost asleep, and that for him the prosaic day is going to continue unmitigated through the entire night.

He struggled to maintain a semblance of equanimity as he took his leave. I'll kiss her goodbye, he thought, and leaned forward to do so. For an instant their faces oscillated from side to side like two opposing magnets pushed together, as each aimed and re-aimed for the wrong cheek. Then Lena disappeared into the darkness of her hallway, and the heavy door clicked shut behind her.

The station was a glare of neon through glass at the end of the dark street. A woman in a white coat, walking toward Steven, crossed over to the other pavement. The gesture seemed to taunt him with his harmlessness. He fumbled in his wallet for his ticket.

The last Métro would only take him as far as Étoile. From there he would have to walk, or take a taxi (yes, the hundred-franc notes were still zippered safely away). The train stank of sulfur. Grime, clotted into the pores of his hands, had begun to make his palms and fingers feel swollen and itchy, so that all he wanted to do was plunge them into a basin of water, then sleep and forget.

Already the evening had begun to recede into unreality. What survived of that brush with danger to prove it had occurred? A missing button! A sob of involuntary laughter shook him as he remembered that. And of Lena what survived? The blond hair came to mind, the red trousers, the beige cardigan, the voice lowing, "How *lovely*, how *exciting*," but the face? He tried to summon that clear smiling face, but could not. All that materialized was a blurred Nordic archetype devoid of distinction, and though as a fact he could recall a slight squareness of jaw, and a faint blemish in the white of one eye, the whole face—Lena herself—continued to elude him. That made him feel vicious; it was as if he had spent the evening addressing a cipher in some purely internal argument, and nothing of Lena herself, whoever she was, had been allowed to interrupt.

He was hot and arid in the rime of his own dried sweat, longing for moisture and sleep, and still more for the comfort of another voice. Then realized the only voice that could give him this comfort was Gloria's, and he had betrayed her so thoroughly in thought if not in deed that he felt too ashamed to resurrect, even in imagination, her calm, reassuring tones. That was the worst of it; to have fallen from grace without so much as a spurt of pleasure in the falling. The justice of the weak, he thought, catching his miserable-looking face in the carriage window.

He wrenched the door open at Étoile, and spat on his hands to moisten then, but only succeeded in making them feel grimier. Few people had got off the train, and by the time Steven reached the blue and white *Sortie* notice at the end of the platform there was no one in sight.

Neon light was harsh on the beige-tiled walls, and the hot, stale air tasted of the million lungs it had coursed through that day. A paper chase of *Sortie* notices led Steven up a steep flight of stairs, along a corridor lined with black bulls wearing chefs' hats—*Goutez au Boeuf Pampa*—up another stairway flanked by a frozen escalator, on through a chamber where the advertisements were all papered over in black, then through some forbidding metal doors that opened narrowly with a pneumatic hiss.

Here the beige tiles gave way to a still less yielding white mosaic, and the exits divided into two general directions. Was it Foch or Hoche he wanted? Foch, he decided, and headed left, where the arrow pointed to avenues Carnot, de la Grande-Armée, and Foch. He noticed a light go out to his right, and heard a man's voice saying, "*Allons y.*" Then there was a sound of footsteps receding toward the Champs-Élysées exit.

His hands were getting hotter and drier as he walked along the empty twisting tunnel. They stung now, rather than itched.

In an effort to take his mind from himself, he observed carefully the impenetrable iconography of the subway. What were those thin trenches on either side of the tunnel floor? Why was the ceiling railed with metal slats and why were some of the slats buckled? He counted fourteen advertisements for Greek holidays. At the end of the corridor was an exit, but to Wagram, not Foch.

He quickened his pace, impatient to be out of this maze. More stairs led him down to another, dimmer, corridor. Here the trenches were tiled over, and there were no ceiling slats. Yugoslavia, *Un grain de beauté entre le ciel et la mer*, was recommended. He wondered, as the corridor twisted round, with again no prospect of ending, whether he had perhaps made a mistake in not following the voices out of the Champs-Élysées exit.

He came then to another empty chamber, colored in a violent tessellated pattern of red and orange glazed hexagons. Here some of the neon tubes were flickering, which gave a sense at once of activity and cold lifelessness to the estranging polished steel shapes of ticket barriers, hermetic litter bins, rows of escalator heads. . . . An illuminated sign saying *Information* stood before an invincible steel-shuttered kiosk. Off to the right, through some glass doors, was the exit to the Avenue Carnot. Steven decided to get out here, but each of the glass doors was locked.

How absurd, Steven thought, shrinking back from them. He was almost running as he left the chamber. His mouth, now, was parched too, though his bladder, he realized, was uncomfortably full; and dust, not blood, seemed to be swelling his hands.

The mottled flame pattern gave way, in the next tunnel, to an icy, splintering arrangement of whites, grays, and blues, like the dazzle pattern on a battleship. This tunnel was the longest yet, and even by running, Steven felt he was making no progress to its end. A minor-looking exit, which he did not stop to investigate, led off to the Avenue de la Grande-Armée.

The beginnings of a fury against the French began to stir in Steven's mind, as a sign directed him along yet another long and vacant corridor. This one was noticeably shabbier than the rest. Butt ends and tissues were scattered over the floor. Sections of the wall had crumbled, or been pulled away, and lay as rubble over the mysterious trenches. Huge blisters of cream paint swelled above the layer of once more dull white tiling. *Lima, Delhi, Lima, New York, Delhi, Lima, Marrakesh (1,150f.)* flashed by, then nothing but white, and there at the end, pointing up some stairs, was a sign marked *Avenue Foch.*

As Steven bounded toward the steps, the ceiling hid fewer and fewer of them, until the top became visible. And drawn right across the top was a reticulated steel door of the type you are warned to guard your fingers against in lifts.

Steven had to steady himself against the wall as he turned around to reenter the labyrinth. It dawned on him that the place was no longer one of transit, but of destination. Only for a night, but it was like glimpsing your corner in eternity—the cold light deadening all it illuminated, the scenery at once hostile and familiar. . . . All that fathomless, lifeless intention, that mechanical activity. The only hope was that one of the exits in the Champs-Élysées direction had been left open.

He could feel the lactic acid burning his muscles as he set them in action again. Sweat trickled over his lips, aggravating his thirst, which he felt almost less on his tongue than in his desiccated palms.

He raced back along the corridor, barely in control of his legs, which at one point sent him sprawling onto a heap of dusty rubble covering the thin gutter. As he sat there, choking with misery, and nursing a whitened knee-graze where a stone had scuffed through his pressed gray trousers, he saw, gleaming from the gutter, a thin line of some liquid residue. He knelt forward and edged his hands sideways into the gutter. For an instant, contact with the cool moisture was blissful. Then it began to sting, and as he raised his hands to investigate, he smelled bleach, and started frantically wiping his hands on his blue shirt, ruining it, and doing little to alleviate the pain. His stupidity would have been comical, even to him, had it not issued from such desperation.

Another steel grille blocked the exit to the Avenue de la Grande-Armée. He staggered past, burning at every jointure and extremity; past the chamber with the information kiosk and the locked glass doors to Avenue Carnot, past Yugoslavia, Greece, another hatted bull recommending its own flesh . . . until he came to the place where the two sets of exits divided into opposite directions.

There were some phone booths here. Catching sight of the blue and yellow international dialing code notices, Steven stopped in his tracks. He could phone Gloria and tell her everything. Her forgiveness would make a mere purgatory of this hell. He began to dial but was overwhelmed by a sudden sense of foreboding; there would be no answer, or a man's voice would answer: he imagined Delmore making some glib, embarrassed jest—*No hard feelings, huh? Did you check out Lena?*—and he let the receiver fall back on its hook.

He walked away cautiously, as if he thought he might catch an open exit unawares. Six glass doors led to Avenue Wagram. One was locked. Steven pushed hesitantly at another, dreading it. It too was locked, and he fled without testing the others, down through another warren of tunnels and stairs and blocked exits, until he came to the large ticket hall serving the suburban lines.

This too was deserted, but it felt not quite so dead. The scale and decor were bigger and brasher; it seemed perceptibly more connected to the aboveground world.

A sign pointed down a corridor to the Champs-Élysées exit.

Still parched and aching and covered in white powder from the rubble, Steven half ran, half walked, down through bilious green and yellow concentric diamonds patterning the corridor. There were no glass doors at the end; only a flight of cement steps, and beside them a stairless escalator shaft full of cables that looked like vast dried entrails. No steel grille barred access to the pavement.

Steven leaped up the stairs three at a time. He was almost screaming for breath when he reached the top. He emerged facing the Arc de Triomphe and he reeled toward it, gasping. A group of tourists who had seen him emerge skirted slowly past him, looking at him with a mixture of suspicion and contempt, then lost interest and hurried on toward their hotel on the Champs-Élysées.

Dead Labor

SUMMER, and my mentor lay in hospital. I was apprehensive about visiting him. I had done things I ought not to have done, and left undone those things that I . . . I was neglecting my duty, yes, joining the rats.

I realized the extent of my dereliction as I set off to visit him one moist, breezeless afternoon. I tried to summon an image of his face, but my summons was met with a blur; a blur topped with a great hank of absolutely black hair, but a blur all the same. I thought of my admiration for the man, my gratitude and affection. These, undeniably, were my feelings for Samuelson, but they lay quite comatose.

I tried to prod them into life.

I began to observe my surroundings as Samuelson would have had me observe them. There was plenty here for the Samuelson vision of life. The long road was flanked by a colossal and classically ravaged housing estate. Children were playing in pits full of smashed glass and excrement. This was Samuelson's melancholic England. It could have been an extension of one of his stage sets; mothers in floral housecoats sitting on the mean terraces contemplating suicide. . . .

I hurried past the place. It was having no effect on me, and I switched it off as you switch off a favorite piece

89

of music heard once too often. I did not want it to be spoiled forever.

The sky was pavement gray with a shapeless lemony stain in it, just too bright to look at. Miniature irises with remnants of petals the same lemon color grew against a wall, their triangles of dead flowers resembling burnt-out catherine wheels. Laburnum corals, too, were turning from yellow to an ugly brown. These small corruptions drew my mind away from Samuelson. All along the side of the hospital were huge horse chestnut trees in full flower, multitudes of deep crimson blossoms showing through the dark leaves, each one like . . . like . . . like a . . .

. . . like a giant mulberry, a marzipan tree, like the excised innards of a glass paperweight . . . I was looking into metaphor and simile. My new friend Philippa was indirectly to thank, or blame, for this. My new friend Philippa had stirred me in a way that urchins and ravaged housing estates no longer seemed to. She was to thank, or blame, for much. She was Gardening, Antiques, and Restaurants for a new magazine about to be launched at income groups A and AB. She was looking for people to write for her; I was looking for work, Samuelson's Open Theater Project no longer funded and no longer functioning since the second month of his absence. She offered me Restaurants, and in a fit of gallantry I swore that she and she alone would be "my guest," "my friend," "my companion," wherever I dined in the name of her magazine.

After the party, I dropped her at her flat in Wandsworth. She repeated her offer; I, my oath. I drove away into the quiet night watching the great breweries and power stations reel in and out of my rearview mirror; feeling, as my car sped me across the Thames and through Chelsea, the peculiar vibrancy of an illicit joy to which guilt will attach itself but has not yet done so.

A formal commission arrived from Philippa on the day before I visited Samuelson. Three restaurants, two thousand words, budget £200, fee £200, to be delivered in three weeks. Scribbled in ballpoint beneath were the words: "Ring me soonest. My mouth is watering already! Love Philippa XXX."

Ring me soonest. The affection excited me, the affectation made me wince. The task too, suddenly a reality, attracted and repelled me in equal measures. To write that kind of thing, and for that kind of magazine . . . but then the money, and the food, and then Philippa herself . . .

I bought the glossies and spent the afternoon immersed in banquets, balls, and the sundry other pursuits of income groups A and AB. I read with detachment, holding in check my Samuelsonian distaste for this world, in an effort to learn how to write for its creatures. An appreciation of the nuances of class, an allusion pitched just within bounds of the knowledge guaranteed by a private education, an amusing coinage—all these were prized. But the stylistic commodity most highly valued of all was the surprising simile, the ingenious metaphor. These were delivered with superlative dash; the author knew that here, if nowhere else, he or she was giving readers a proper return on their investment—an echo of the satisfactions of a good business deal where two items were had for the price of one. *My bream came in a faintly yellow creamy sauce flecked all over with green herbs, as if it had been dressed by Laura Ashley.* Olé!

A fractional stirring of the air caused one of the crimson chestnut flowers to topple through the branches. I picked it up as I entered the hospital, and saw how here, too, the pristine color was beginning to turn.

A nurse showed me to a small annex off one of the men's wards. I stood in the doorway and looked for the thick black swatch of Samuelson's hair. I couldn't see it. I was about to go away and ask again for his ward, when I heard my name called. The voice was Samuelson's, but the head it came from bore no immediate resemblance to his. The face was sucked in around the contours of the skull. The skin was bloodless. An egg-sized patch of darkness surrounded each eye. His hair was white, and stood up in sparse sprouts, areas of scalp visible beneath them, the whole thing altogether like a half-blown dandelion clock.

His right arm protruded, naked and white, from the side of the bed. I'd seen this arm reach down and hoist to the safety of a platform a woman bloodied by a bottle at a rally. It looked now as if the weight of the bedside glass would snap it. Sticking into what remained of the bicep was a needle attached by a tube to a plastic drip-feed bag half full of a clear liquid.

"All it lacks is a goldfish. . . ." he said, looking up at the bag. A timpani of rattling phlegm accompanied his words. I smiled for him and kept my mouth shut. There was so much I wanted to avoid telling him.

"I gather we've lost our grant."

I nodded.

"You must have a—excuse me"—he broke off to dribble into a wad of tissues—"a lot of time on your hands now."

"I suppose I do." Would he question me, and if he did, would I be able to lie to him? He could be a formidable inquisitor. I wanted to go before I was forced to witness those cavernous eyes absorb and echo back whatever deceits and evasions I might address to them.

"I wonder if you would do me a favor?"

"Of course," I said, relieved.

He raised himself up slowly, and took from his bedside table some pieces of paper covered with notes.

"I was asked a while ago to write something about my work for an anthology of essays on politics and theater. I wasn't all that interested. But I said I'd give it some thought—you know—when I had time. . . ." He paused to regain his breath, then went on to tell me that he had decided to produce a statement for posterity, that he was at the moment too weak to write anything but fragmentary notes, and that he considered me the one person capable of turning his notes into a presentable essay.

"They wrote a week ago, saying I had another month if I wanted to get in the book. That would give you about three weeks. . . ."

He passed me the papers. There was a heading, "Dead Labor," followed by the quotation from Marx: "Capital is dead labor which, vampire-like, lives only by sucking living labor, and lives the more, the more labor it sucks."

I looked at Samuelson, feeling my sense of relief turn to unease. Two months ago, one month even, this task would have presented no difficulties. Now, however, it appeared distinctly problematic. To do it at the same time as the magazine piece would require me to split myself into two irreconcilable frames of mind. Something told me I should try to duck out of it. But I had immense obligations to this man—for a long time almost everything I valued in myself could be attributed to his influence. I had yet to judge whether I had drifted clean away from this influence, or was merely on holiday from it. Either way, he was calling in a debt. No means of evading it came to mind, short of a flat refusal, and I was too much in awe of him for that. My tongue was enslaved to the forms of politeness.

"It looks very interesting," I heard myself say.

We discussed the details. I promised to return in a fortnight with a preliminary draft, and left him crackling and wheezing on his bed, like an ill-tuned radio.

My companion's Steak Ambassadeur was delicious. No. My companion's Steak Ambassadeur was of a tenderness so exquisite you could have—

"What's that you're writing now?" asked Ringmesoonest with an impish grin.

I looked up from my jotting pad. "Secret," I whispered. She made a play of grabbing for the pad, but I snatched it away, tut-tutting her.

"Tell me or I'll scream."

"Oh, all right then: My companion's . . . my companion tossed back a large brandy with her customary brio, extinguished her cigar, and staggered to her feet, saying, 'My place, honey. I'm gonna ride you ragged.' "

Ringmesoonest laughed a tinkling laugh. She didn't; her laughter aspired halfheartedly to the condition of tinkling. She knew what she was doing. She had a passing attraction to me, and was happy to let her gestures refer to the flirtatious premise on which this attraction was based, in order to help it flourish. Everything about her could be read as a series of concessions—her precision-cut hair, her seamless charm, her big brown eyes with their perfectly white whites, the endless variety of smiles that played on her face, each one showing you something new to like in her lips or cheeks; her pale throat, the discretion of her scent. . . . These things mean nothing to me, her manner suggested, they're all yours, only let me have what I want of you in return.

A waiter came to remove our plates. Another joined him to replenish my glass with wine from the silver bucket beside me. A third hovered behind him with a menu in his hand. It excited us, all that attention, made us into a source of energy as if we were living under a new decree where it was the candle that fed off the moths and not vice versa.

A feeling of power crept into me as I read the menu; a little rush of magnanimity, as if I were up above the world and could order anything: *I'll have Chartres, please, and the Guggenheim. My friend would like Mauritius.* . . . I recognized it as a corrupt sensation. I let it bloom in me, observing it like a scientist at a controlled explosion. A necklace of condensation on the ice bucket broke, and the beads streaked down the silver surface. It struck me that Samuelson was dying. I passed momentarily into crisis. I felt like someone awaking in a room altogether different from the one he went to sleep in. What was I doing here? Who was this girl? The myth of intimacy that had wrapped itself around us seemed suddenly to be disintegrating. I felt cold and exposed. I vowed to myself that I would start work on Samuelson's piece tomorrow morning; no, tonight.

How was our myth patched up? By glass after glass of wine and brandy? Partly, but also by the sensitivity with which she adapted herself to my shift of mood. She became quiet now, and engaged me in serious conversation. She asked me about my work with Samuelson. I had a faint feeling of unease, talking about him to her, but she listened with such absorption and concern that I soon found myself telling her all about his life and how I had come into it. I mentioned also the task he had given me.

"I must get it started tonight."

It all made her feel so frivolous, she said in a soft, pensive voice. I took her at her word and told her that I, for one, thought she was very far from frivolous. I felt a tremendous affection for her, and great relief at having recovered so precious and pleasant a feeling.

I drove her across the river to her door. She asked me in. Her flat was leafy and cushiony, trinkets everywhere, perfume atomizers, scarves, records, bracelets, a printer's tray on the wall with a little ornament in every niche, masses of patterned fabrics, a bentwood hat tree in full, exotic fruit. There was a coal fire too, facing the sofa. A pinkish glow peeped through cracks in the blanket of white ash.

"Summer fire," I remarked.

"I know, but it's pretty. You could revive it if you like. There's more coal in the scuttle. I'll get some drinks. . . . "

She went into the kitchen. I heard the creak of ice being prized from its tray as I blew on the coals, and the clink of ice in glass as I tipped the smooth black ovoids from the scuttle into the fire. The old ash fell away. The fresh coal reflected the red light of the embers, and slowly the reflection became the thing itself, blazing out brighter than the weakening originals.

We drank gins rapidly on the sofa, talking a little nervously, but sure of our ground. The fire became an orange sea with diminishing black islands in it, thin bluish flames playing overhead. I took her hand. The hand squeezed mine, though its owner affected not to have noticed.

"Look," she said, and with her free hand tossed the ice cubes and slice of lemon from her tumbler into the fire. A spectacular plume of steam hissed out. The sea shimmered. Patches of darkness were sucked in around each gleaming nugget of ice as it sapped the heat from the coals in its melting. The lemon slice writhed, shriveled, and released a sweet citric scent in its candle-flame apotheosis. She put down her glass and leaned toward me with her eyes wide open looking into mine; conceding to me, as we kissed, all her softness and charm, her pale throat and discreet scent, the white whites and deep brown pupils of her eyes, her repertoire of smiles . . . a warm tumbling of herself into me, so it felt. We lay there kissing, growing blood-heavy and languid under each other's touch. The coals in the fire had recovered from their icy assault and were now a single golden mass, so that, as jackets, blouse, trousers, skirt, fell away from us, we felt the brazier heat directly on our skins and glowed like coals ourselves in its reflection. She lay naked in my arms, light and delicate, an exquisite instrument taken from the plush-lined mold of its case, a faint trace of amusement on her lips to remind me as I caressed her that all this was provisional, transactional. She was almost passive in her enjoyment: receptive, glazed in her own sensations, feeding delicately on me. A pink blush rose on her pale cheeks. She pressed my mouth gently to her nipple, and then brought me into her, closing her eyes. Her breathing stayed quiet as it grew faster and higher in pitch, and when she came she did so in one silent, extended, blissful, private shimmer.

Traffic sounded in the distance. A clock ticked in the bedroom.

After a while she disentangled herself from me and went to run a bath.

"What about Mr. Samuelson?" she asked as she left the room. There was no mockery in her voice, but I felt mocked. It was three in the morning. The notes were all at my place and I could do nothing without them. I wondered if this was her way of telling me to go. But then she shouted from the bathroom, "There's only enough hot for one. Shall I leave you my water?"

Samuelson, I decided, would do much better by me in the morning.

I lay in the warm, soapy water, sponging myself with her sponge, feeling happy and satiated. She was much lovelier than I had imagined. I could feel her presence in my mind, a warm soft radiance.

As I climbed sleepily from the bath, I caught a whiff of her perfume on my skin. Her large, damp towel carried the same fragrance, and as I dried myself I could sense it impregnating me like the subtlest of varnishes, a sheen of Philippa's existence enclosing my own.

No accident that textures of fringe stage predom. matt while W. End stage aims glitter & shine. Impression given of massive industry, what sparkles is labor-intensive. Forests & millennia required to crystallize one seam of diamonds. (Adam Smith on rel. value of water & diamonds) . . .

The notes were square on the desk before me, illumi-nated by a beam of bright midday sunlight. On one side of them was a green mug of steaming coffee. On the other side was my portable typewriter, a piece of crisp white paper wound about its roller. I sat there marshaling my thoughts, feeling confident in my power to execute this task. Whenever I moved, a hint of Philippa's scent rose from me, filling me with rich, pleasurable sensations that in turn seemed to fill everything inanimate around me with glimmerings of benevolent life: the green mug with its dancing genie of steam, the Olivetti's dial of levers waiting to transform thought into print—an occult conspiracy to make me feel loved and intimately connected with the world. I looked up, and tried to shape the first sentence in my mind. I was getting there, and had my fingers poised above the keys, when the telephone rang.

It was Philippa's boss, a cajoling male voice speaking with an expression I recognized at once as simulated deference. He was awfully sorry to disturb me only they'd had a crisis at the magazine and he wondered if I would do him a favor. The chap doing the Nightlife and New Openings pages had dropped out, and they needed someone urgently to give them copy. Philippa'd said . . .

I sensed danger in this voice, and kept quiet. It began to flatter me now, its owner interpreting my silence as reluctance. "She says you're exactly the man for us. I have this good feeling about you." The words filled me with panic. I made noises of uncertainty, but he pressed on. "It should be a lot of fun for you. Do it myself if I had the time. Free tickets to everything—discos, cocktail bars, new restaurants on top of the ones you're doing for us anyway. . . . Actually I've had my secretary post you a batch of invites. Go to them all. We just need a few sentences on each one—glorified listings really. Won't take you any time. Pay you over the odds, of course. Money for old rope between you and me. . . ."

I felt cornered. There was a vague threat floating on

his words; a shadow of something cast just too faintly to be identifiable. "We're gambling on Philippa's say-so, of course, but I have a hunch about you"—an intimation of knowledge that somehow gave him power. "We'd like you to get yourself known a bit—be a sort of man about town. We'll print a card for you. . . ." I could feel myself submitting to him, like a creature entering metamorphosis, powerlessly witnessing its familiar shape mutating into something new and strange. . . .

"What d'you say to it, then?"

"Hm. Okay. Yes. Thank you. I'd love to. It's very kind of you to ask me."

"Good. Now here's a surprise: your first assignment's in an hour. Philippa's waiting for you at a new lunch revue place in Fulham. She can do it herself if you absolutely can't make it. I think you should, though. . . ."

The chestnut blossoms had succumbed to summer. Crimson petals had shriveled away to reveal antlers of stem that made me think of Philippa's bentwood hat tree. I saw emblems of her wherever I went. Over the past two weeks she had become installed inside me. She was no longer so much a source of pleasure as a prerequisite for it. I was abandoning myself to her. A thimble's worth of me was watching it happen, unable to do anything about it.

Three days after the lunch date in Fulham, I had slunk reluctantly back into my room. A bruise of turquoise mold had risen on the scum of milk fat riding the unconsumed coffee. No miracle had occurred, translating the notes into formal prose on the piece of typing paper now warped around the shape of the roller. The task awaited me still. I forced myself to sit down and concentrate. My ears—all my senses—were still ringing with the weekend's excess of free drinking and dancing with Philippa, of making love on the sofa with an escalating urgency and passion. . . . We had become a *perpetuum mobile* of arousal and appeasement. We would abandon, midflight, the simplest of domestic tasks as desire seized us, and fall back together, tugging at buttons, zippers, laces, clasps, fasteners. . . . Continually radiant in my mind's eye was an afterglow of tumbling body forms—cloven spheres, softened cylinders—a cubist kaleidoscope of Philippa that sometimes occluded everything else around me.

"Dead Labor" . . . How difficult it all looked; how impossibly complex the world it postulated. Would I ever be able to think my way back into Samuelson's theories of drama, his vision of theater as an economic microcosm where new forms of living could be experimented with like shapes and spaces in an architect's model? That thimble's worth of me tried valiantly to lead the way. It was as unappealing a prospect as drinking the cold, rancid coffee beside it would have been. By a stupendous effort of will I managed to become Samuelson for one, two, three sentences. I then sat back, exhausted. That was the worst over, I told myself. But my conscience was still nagging me. To appease it, I set to work on my restaurant notes. I had the same obligations here, after all.

What a contrast this work was! Far from distracting me, my tape loop of breasts and thighs and moss mounds of dark brown pubic hair seemed to be *generating* the stream of words that now slipped out of me. *My companion's Steak Ambassadeur was of a tenderness so exquisite you could happily have fed it to a toothless infant.* . . .

So it continued—a week and more of sipping A to Z

through cocktail menus, of dressing up to dance under searchlights or strobe lights, of undressing to make love and sleep stickily in the musky sheets of Philippa's bed, of cramming our bellies with pâté en croute, hot fruit soups, ocean creatures in aspic, surprises, bombes, sukiyaki, chicken in chocolate, sea slugs, fish lips, duck webs, calf heels . . . of lying all day in a kimono, half stupefied, while Philippa went out to work.

Three or four times, my former self reared its head above this sweet miasma of sensations, and I raced home full of guilt and good intention. But as soon as I was sitting before Samuelson's notes, the impulse would always ebb away. A tortured sentence or two might trickle out, and I would end up once more appeasing my conscience with a review or a listing. *The only creatures likely to feel at home in Lulu's Kitchen are dysentery bacilli. . . .*   Slick, glib little gobbets that spurted out of me like—ah, no . . .

A doctor in a white coat was adjusting Samuelson's plastic drip-feed bag as I entered the annex. Patients and visitors were murmuring quietly together. I felt numb and distant, sealed off from the place as if I or it were enclosed in thick aquarium glass. Samuelson was flat on his back. His hair was even whiter and thinner. One more puff and it would all be gone. The shadows around his eyes seemed to have entered deep into the pigment of his skin. The protruding arm was skeletal.

"Good of you to come." His voice was scarcely more than a whisper.

I smiled and said as little as possible. As long as my bubble remained intact, I was safe. I'd brought the piece of paper with my few sentences on it. I had no plan.

"Did you . . . did you get anywhere with those notes, then?"

The timidity was out of character. It was the tone of a man relinquishing his claim on others. I could see that Samuelson had moved, in two weeks, from a central to a peripheral relation with the living world.

I began to formulate an excuse, but couldn't summon the conviction to see it through. I showed him my piece of paper.

"I did a little. Not very much. I'm sorry."

His eyes flickered from me to the paper, and back again.

"Too busy on your own work, I suppose."

"Yes," I said, "that sort of thing."

"Well . . . good. You look healthy on it."

There was a silence while he read my sentences, and a silence after he'd finished them. I was trembling.

"I will get it done," I said.

"There's only a week. . . ."

"I know. I'll do it, though. I'll bring it here and we can go over it, then I'll take it straight to the publisher's myself."

"Will you? That's kind." He closed his eyes. I stayed a moment, looking for signs of activity in the drip-feed bag, imagining it as the sac of a giant tick with a grotesquely long proboscis, not feeding Samuelson, but sucking out the glass-clear essence of him. I rose, and left him sleeping peacefully.

There is a passage in Freud's essay "On the Universal Tendency to Debasement in the Sphere of Love" describing psychical impotence. The victim "reports that he has a feeling of an obstacle inside him, the sensation of a counter-will which successfully interferes with his conscious intention."

My conscious intention was to write the piece for Samuelson. Morning after morning I would see Philippa off to work, and sit down before the notes, which I had now transferred to her flat. Time after time I read them through, and each time the meanings they dealt with seemed more remote from me than ever. Even so, I should have been able to perform. I was not required to understand or create arguments, merely to articulate them in clear English. But I could not do it. A paralyzing lassitude came over me every time I tried; an inertia that was not indolence but a powerful negating force—an antimagnetism that made myself and the notes mutually repellent.

"Where they love," continues Freud, "they do not desire, and where they desire they cannot love."

We awoke late and bleary-eyed on the morning of the sixth day. Philippa was staring at me listlessly as I opened my eyes. I detected minute signals of hostility. I rolled over to embrace her, unreproved if undesired. . . . At breakfast she hardly spoke. Her silence made me unnaturally talkative. I could sense my words grating on her, but I kept chattering.

"I *must* get Samuelson done by this evening," I said.

She turned away.

I sat down at her writing table with the notes. Tomorrow was the deadline for both pieces. The reviews and listings were all but done. This evening an old friend of Philippa's was opening a nightclub—a small once-a-week place with dancing, seafood, and some sort of cabaret. The idea was for me to write it up as the final listing on my Nightlife page, immediately after it was over, and send the completed copy with Philippa to the magazine the following morning.

I heard her cleaning up the kitchen as I read once

more through Samuelson's notes. Shortly afterward, she moved into the drawing room with a spherical Hoover in tow. It began to hum resonantly. I pretended to be undisturbed, but the drone of the machine was mesmerizing me, emptying me of thought. I turned around and stared at it gliding smoothly behind Philippa as she moved, stopping when she stopped, filling itself with the dust three weeks had milled from our bodies and possessions.

"Am I disturbing you?" She said it sharply, and before I could stop myself, I replied in kind, "Don't you have to go to work?"

"I'm taking the day off. Is that all right or would you prefer me to leave?"

"I'm sorry." I turned back to the piece.

She abandoned the Hoover and marched into the bedroom. The silence she bequeathed was as disturbing as the noise had been. I went into the room. She was lying on the bed, staring at the ceiling and chewing her lip ruminatively. I knelt by her and put my hand on her shoulder. She smiled wanly without looking at me. I slid my hand from her shoulder to her breast. She lay immobile for a moment while I squeezed it. Then she exploded—"*Get* off!"—and recoiled to the other side of the bed. I left the room stunned, as much by my own gesture as by her reaction. I looked at the notes, but I might as well have been looking at a tablet engraved with hieroglyphs.

I went back into the bedroom, to propitiate. My reception was warmer than I might have expected. She was not a callous person; she would not abandon an affair without first examining it for signs of life. We embraced, and kissed fondly, struggling out of our clothes. She twisted herself tightly around me, kissing me methodically all over, as if searching for ingress back into our former intimacy. There was a frenziedness in our movement, and a hopelessness too. Something was wrong; each time one of us rose to a pitch of desire, the other would go dead, cold, flaccid. Thus we stopped and started, and broke off again for cigarettes, gin, air . . . until at last we rolled apart, sweaty and frustrated, miserably defeated by a fact which neither of us had willed into existence, but which was unassailable.

We spent the afternoon in considerate silence, avoiding each other, as far as this was possible in her small flat. We had had our fill of each other; that was the fact. We were like two swollen drops of rain on a windowpane: if we so much as touched, we would fall and disintegrate.

I sat staring at the white wall above the notes, waiting for the night, a prey to one sensation after another. I would feel weak, then angry, then a current of sexual desire would travel through me, the sweet blood collecting at my groin dispersed in turn by a sudden irradiation of guilt about Samuelson. Where did these feelings come from? I appeared to have no control over them at all; to be no more than a receptacle, a vacuum into which they strayed at random. I wondered how far into my psyche this principle extended; were my rational faculties—my opinions, beliefs, interests—after all as haphazard and involitional as my emotions, and did they share the same mysterious provenance? What was the essence of this creature leaning on a table in a darkening room, what was its irreducible quality? I sat still, probing its archaeology, passing layer after layer of superimposed ideas, acquired mannerisms, mimicry repeated until it felt like personal conviction. . . . I was merciless, inquisitorial: I saw the mildew of corruption everywhere; nothing was untainted, or if anything was, it was no more than that

minute lost particle of life you wake up to in the small
hours, panicking at its insubstantiality. . . .

The place was hot and crowded, dimly lit. We settled
into a table with half a dozen of Philippa's friends. I had
the impression she knew everybody there, had known
them all her life. It was quite a network—A and AB
at leisure. Groups of them in gorgeous colors milling
between tables, bar, dance floor; dispersing, regroup-
ing . . .

The young proprietor came over to us, a bottle of
champagne in each hand. He crossed the bottles around
Philippa's neck and bent over her, searching for her lips.
Afterward he took my hand in both of his, greeting me
like a long-lost friend.

Glasses were brought, and we held them up in a bright
cluster to collect the overspill of foam, the cuckoo spit.
At the back of the room a waiter in a white coat was
shucking oysters and stacking them on beds of crushed
ice. Deep-pink sides of smoked salmon were laid out
along a table, between sunflowers with king prawns for
petals and caviar for seeds. There was a tank with long
sea trout speeding to and fro in it. Another with lobsters
and giant crayfish, snouted, plated, bristling with spines
and wiry antennae; prehistoric. Colored lights shone
from within the tanks, submarine blues and greens on
coral trees and arches of rock. Silver bubbles streamed
from a plastic tube immersed in the water.

I gulped my champagne, feeling the sting of its fizz on
the roof of my mouth. Aqueous light and a boom of
music pulsed from the dance floor. Philippa went off to
dance with Baz, a gaunt-faced man wearing purple
shoes. Her friends tried to include me in the talk. They'd

heard I was reviewing the place, and traded comic send-ups of the kind of thing I might write. They saw I wasn't listening, though, and left me alone in my corner.

I had the notes with me. I took them surreptitiously from my pocket, and unfolded them under the edge of the table. I was drinking steadily; every time I picked up my glass it had been refilled. People came and went with plates of seafood. A pile of oyster shells grew in the cen-ter of our table—stiffened frills, a tang of brine. . . . Noise came in waves, swelling and receding. Time was streaming out. I wrote: "There seems also a more than symbolic significance in our society's preferred method of neutralizing its most toxic waste—by converting it into a form of glass." Then I scribbled as a memo for the morning: "Cross a mermaid with a rhinoceros and you'll have an idea what I mean when I say the crayfish here are *giant* . . ."

Philippa was still dancing with Baz. I heard waves crashing on a pebble shore—a background tape just au-dible in the occasional lull. The sound filled me with sadness. I was losing touch with the party. A curtain by our table was opened to reveal a stage. Philippa came back sparkling with secret exuberance. Someone sang a song on the stage. Jugglers and fire swallowers followed. The men at my table hooted their appreciation and stamped their feet. They were drunk, and I too was drinking myself to the verge of something.

A man with a skull and an undertaker's outfit appeared on the stage. He was part magician, part mime. He mimed stalking a rabbit, then produced from thin air a real rabbit, which he held upside down. It was freshly dead; a drop of dark blood splashed to the floor. I had a feeling of déjà vu, and a sense, too, of foreboding. He was going to ask for an assistant. I tried to make myself invisible. He called out the names of a dozen guests and asked them to check their pockets. He'd picked them all earlier on. The victims filed up sheepishly to collect wallets, checkbooks, and so forth. One or two of them looked faintly nettled, but he had the power of the audience on his side.

He produced a tabloid newspaper. There was no print on the pages. He mimed bafflement, exasperation, fury —tearing the paper in half again and again, ripping it to shreds while the audience roared with laughter. He folded all the pieces into a little wad, tapped it with his white-gloved hand, then unfolded it. It had become a creased but perfectly intact copy of the *Daily Mail.* Quelling the applause, he announced that he was going to teach the trick to a member of the audience. He scanned us with his skull face, sprang down from the stage, and made straight for me.

"You, sir, I wonder if you would do me a favor. . . ."

He had a firm grip on my arm, and was pulling me to my feet.

"And bring these pieces of paper with you—yes, yes— bring them along."

There was no disobeying him. I rose and climbed the stage. I was in a glassy champagne trance, far away from the clusters of green-lit faces angled upward at me. Waves broke on shingle in the quietness.

"Do exactly as I do." He had another blank newspaper, which he tore in two. I tore the notes in two. He tore again and I did likewise, again, again. . . . My body was trembling. The wall at the end of the room was like the sail of a giant windmill, slowly revolving. I could see the white-coated waiter clearing up the buffet tables. He flicked a switch by the shellfish tank, cutting the air-feed from the plastic tube. He drew the last crustacean from the tank and dropped it, flailing, into a saucepan behind him. A bald head in the audience caught the green light and sank back into shadow. I could hear a groundswell of laughter.

"Tap your hand like so. Now open it up. . . ."

A chill tingle, a *frisson* of terror, came and went as the shreds of Samuelson's notes fluttered from my hand to the ground. I felt his presence in the room, a ghostly analogue. . . . The laughter rose as the magician jeered at me, waving his own intact paper at the audience. I noticed, as I left the stage, that his shoes were purple.

England's Finest

FRANK AND JILL FOWLER were going up up up in the world.

When the money started at last to pour in from Frank's haulage outfit, they bought an old rectory just outside the village of Chesham. They had it fixed up by a designer friend of Jill's, who knew just what they meant when they said, "Make it look authentic but not like some bloody pub." The new fireplaces were thus built of old bricks, and a thatcher was brought in to disguise the garage extension. The only serious lapse was a Victorian gas lamp, now electrified, which Frank insisted on planting like a totem pole outside the front door. The designer frowned, and they half knew it wasn't quite the thing, but it did make the place feel like a real home, and that, they agreed, was more important than anything else.

Frank was an impatient man, always in a hurry to get through with this stage of his life, so he could move on to the next. The twin phantoms of Want and Tedium pursued him from his childhood, and now he wanted everything, but *everything*, to go right for him and Jill.

Together they set out establishing themselves in the local community. You couldn't call their behavior ingratiating; it was too open for that. Frank built a tennis court and sent Jill on a crash course in cordon bleu cookery. The summer parties they gave were offered bla-

tantly as barter—our lavish hospitality for your friendship. By its very directness, the appeal became invisible,
and worked. With the completion of the pool—it had
soft sides and a floor you could squidge with your toes—
no one could doubt that the Fowlers had arrived.

As soon as they discovered they couldn't have children, they opened, without pause for trauma, proce-
dures for adoption. So it was that Sean Toomey ended
his career as an orphan before his sixteenth month was
up and became Edward Fowler.

He was chosen for the cherubic wisps that curled
about his face, for his bright blue eyes and perfectly
formed lips, for the creaminess of his complexion, and
for the blissful chuckling he made when you shook his
cushiony little hand.

He did not enjoy being Edward Fowler. At the age of
three he discovered the art of the tantrum, and the fact
that certain hard round objects broke loudly when you
threw them at the floor. Frank and Jill had been told
enough about adopted children not to be unduly dismayed. They agreed it would be wise to delay plans for
getting a daughter until the son had come to a more
equable agreement with life, and they engaged a succession of Jacquelines, Moniques, and Fräulein Heidis to
deal with him.

The last of these, a young but motherly Belgian called
Odette, recognized in Edward an ingenuous strategy for
coming to terms with the world by annexing little bits of
it into his own private universe. He had a reliquary in
the form of a small red cupboard by his bed, in which he
stored certain objects of fantastic value to him. Chief
among these were a rhinoceros egg, and Sean—a piece
of flint he had kicked all the way back from the end of
the drive without once landing it in the ditch. Odette

encouraged this propensity; instead of forcing a bedtime story on him each night, she sat calmly smoking Sweet Aftons while he hung from the side of his bed in bat-like contemplation of his talismans. She took him on walks through the muddy common and round the plowed fields beyond, to gather possible additions to the collection. When they returned, they would examine the merits of each object in great detail and, after much discussion, select perhaps one of them—an abandoned wren's nest maybe, or a fragment of willow pattern china, or a leaf that autumn had turned into a piece of filigree lacework.

Edward loved, also, pretending to be dead. He would stagger, mortally wounded, into Odette's room and, after much groaning and agonized clutching at his wounds, collapse dead onto the floor. Odette would then mourn him elaborately, listing the virtues of this brave soldier, telling the misery of those he had left behind, naming the many greatnesses his severed destiny had held in store for him . . . until Edward, overcome by the tragedy of the occasion, would begin to weep bitterly for himself and for his loved ones, and in an effort to restore his spirits would jump up and dance a Belgian jig that Odette had taught him.

Shortly before Edward's seventh birthday, Frank and Jill decided that the time had come to start shaping the boy a little more actively into the kind of son and heir they desired. Odette was discharged. She returned to Belgium, leaving behind a tropical plant which Edward kept, unwatered, on his red cupboard, watching it flag until it looked like a junked umbrella.

A priority in Frank and Jill's plans for Edward was to steer him away from a friendship he was forming with the daughter and two sons of Len Davis, an unpopular, unsavory local farmhand. Snobbery came into it, but it was more complicated than that. The children were well on their way to the bad. The boys were known to the local police—they'd stolen things from the village shop, or poured sugar into the proprietor's petrol tank, or probably both, and more besides. They were older than Edward, and you could see him modeling his style of mischief on their own. His attachment to Beverley had its charming side—they had made a house out of a clump of nut saplings circled with string and carpeted with a velvety mosaic of moss collected from old stumps and rocks—but Frank saw no good would come of it. Discomfiting memories of his own past, and a constant anxiety about the future, made it impossible for him to accept any aspect of the present without extending it across time into all its possible catastrophic. consequences. He could tell Beverley was a chip off the old block; what she innocently provoked in Edward now, she would exploit with all her native cunning in years to come. He could see her conniving with her drunkard father to trap the boy. These things happened; you had to look out for them. . . .

A tea party was arranged for some more suitable children, and strictly not the Davises. But they came anyway, protesting that Edward had invited them, and Jill hadn't quite the heart to turn them away.

How unpleasant it was to recall: the tea table like an airy, dreamy citadel; candlelight flickering on quivering, translucent domes, and on the sugar-frosted rims of crystal cylinders; surf-white sandwiches, spread like ripples across the lake of a silver tray. . . . Then the Davises vandalizing it, smearing their filthy fingers through the jellies and cakes, Chinese-burning the other children till they wept for their mothers, screaming their scatological jokes at one another, and Edward blissfully egging them on . . .

After which he entered a new dimension of anarchy. It was not so much what he did, as the aura of refusal he carried with him about the house. He seemed possessed of some principle of living directly and aggressively opposed to Frank and Jill's, so that he had only to enter a room they were in for them to feel it bristling with antagonism against them. He could set a lamp or a chest of drawers against its master, could make a vase of tiger lilies send out waves of contempt against its mistress. . . . And when he did do something wrong, and was punished for it, he left Frank and Jill feeling as though some part of themselves had been spat upon, and trampled in dirt.

"He's dragging me down," said Frank. "I can feel it inside me like something pulling in my chest. He's going to make me ill. I know it. What *is* the matter with him? If I'd thought things were going to get so bloody awful I'd never have adopted. They should warn you about all this. . . ." He coughed and hit his chest violently. "Edward," he shouted, "Edward, come here."

"Yes," said Edward, slouching round the living room door.

"Come here; I want to tell you something. Listen carefully."

Edward folded himself onto the white leather sofa, his light frame barely dimpling the cushion. He stared past his father at the bottle-glass window as if he could see through it to the screeching farm machine that was tearing errant shoots from a hedge, which he could not.

"Pay attention now." Eyes shifted focus lazily from window to father.

"Do you know what adoption means?"

"Yes," Edward said, looking dreamily back at the window.

"What?"

"Don't know."

"Well, why . . . I'll tell you." The machine ground out a screeching accompaniment to his explanation. "Do you understand?"

A silent nod.

"Well, listen, Edward, you are an adopted child. Now that doesn't mean we don't . . ."

As he began to explain why this meant Edward should be extra-considerate of his parents, he realized that the morality he was trying to invoke was beyond his grasp; that he was floundering in contradiction and absurdity, and that as he floundered, the chairs, the prints, the onyx ashtray, glass coffee table, wax fruit, were all extending Edward's blank expression into a derisive sneer, and that the screeching laughter of the machine outside the window was no more than a piece of demonic ventriloquism. . . .

And Edward merely said, "Is that all you wanted to tell me?"

A hiatus where a crisis should have come, nervous energy tingling in a void . . . "He's dragging me down," Frank said to Jill as they drifted on separate floats randomly across the pool. A tinkle of broken glass rang out from the front of the house.

"Oh, God," Frank groaned, and heaved himself out of the pool.

Small pieces of glass glittered on the gravel at the base of the gas lamp. The front lawn was deserted, but an abandoned racket and tennis ball lay on the drive. The broken panes of the lamp seemed to confer instantly an air of dilapidation upon the house. Frank, plump and white in his trunks, passed a hand through his wisps of black hair and felt he could almost cry. He must have it fixed immediately, cancel the occurrence. Under the box hedge Edward gripped Beverley's hand and they giggled as they watched Frank run indoors. They heard the ting of the phone, and Frank saying to someone, "I don't care how much, get here as quickly as possible. . . ."

The winter term yielded the most spectacular addition yet to Edward's red cupboard. A small silver goblet, shallow like a champagne glass, school arms inscribed at its base, was presented to him for scoring most goals on the junior team. Next winter it would pass to his successor.

Frank and Jill mistook the trophy for a good omen. They wanted to honor it with pride of place on the mantelpiece above the fire. Edward let them, and for a few days a precarious harmony reigned. Tentative gestures of affection were displayed between parents and child. Jill and Frank whispered in bed together that the worst was over at last. . . .

Then a neighbor reported seeing Edward smoking a cigarette on the common with the Davis children. Frank shouted at him, and the next day the cup was gone, given new pride of place in the crammed reliquary. With it went that brief spell of harmony, and once more Frank began saying to Jill, "He's dragging me down, I can feel it inside me. . . ."

The worst did not come, and pass, until the following summer. It was occasioned by the visit of Axel, the younger son of Jill's cousin in Munich. Axel, nearly a year older than Edward, was here to learn some English. Edward was to entertain him, and, it was hoped, to benefit from his German cousin's relative maturity.

But Axel arrived at the airport in a pair of yellow Bermuda shorts and a pink Airtex shirt. He was tall and lithe and walked limp-wristed like a girl. He left a strange smell like cooking kidneys in the bathroom every morning. He drank coffee, and asked for it *mit Schlag*, so that *mit Schlag* became a private joke between him and Jill. And he preferred to make halting conversation with Frank, or play tennis with him, than admire Edward's trophies or play with Edward's toys.

Frank and Jill were utterly charmed with Axel. Frank found in him a focus for all the paternal feelings that Edward had so successfully deflected, and he devoted his holiday to him. He jovially corrected his English, coached his swimming, threw bright shillings in the pool for him to catch and keep, bought him a rod, and took him fishing for roach and bream in the slow wide river beyond the common. Jill brought him slices of cake and cups of coffee. "*Mit Schlag?*" "*Ja ja, mit Schlag.* Ha ha!"

Edward was never directly excluded from these activities, but as the hot days passed, and his sulky refusals to join in took on a predictable consistency, invitations became more and more cursory, until finally they ceased.

Axel perceived, and began to exploit, the tensions between parents and son. After meals, when Edward refused to clear the dishes, Axel would assume an expression of simple goodness, and clear them himself. When Edward, in a fit of pique, scrawled abuse across a page of Axel's English phrase book, Axel trotted with it tearfully to Frank and stood sniveling beside him while he berated his son. And in the evenings, when Edward returned home from playing with the Davis children, Axel, sitting snugly between Frank and Jill on the sofa, would look at him with an expression that said clearly, "Look at me. I am the son they always wanted."

"Do try and behave a bit more like Axel, dear. I know it's difficult . . ." said Jill, but these invidious comparisons served only to add fuel to Edward's smoldering sulks.

And one day, shortly before Axel was due to depart, real flames burst up into the afternoon sky. A haystack in a nearby field caught fire and curdled the clear air about it into a dense white cloud of smoke. Men rushed from the farm with rakes and buckets of water to prevent the flames from spreading to the unharvested field alongside. A fire engine came clattering along the unsurfaced road and turned the blazing stack into an ugly heap of wet black ash bristling here and there with yellow tufts of unburnt hay. The local policeman arrived on his bicycle and started asking questions; somebody remembered seeing four children dashing onto the road from a footpath that led through this farm. . . .

Hearing this, Frank and Jill, who had brought Axel with them to see the blaze, exchanged brief, frightened looks, and slipped away with their charge. They said nothing to each other on the subject, sharing an assumption that the best method of keeping the unpalatable at bay was to refuse to acknowledge it. At home, they waited in broody silence for the arrival of Edward.

Axel was the very soul of tact; he tiptoed about doing little chores, and at teatime, when Jill handed him his coffee, he gave her a grave look which tacitly accepted that now was no time for *mit Schlag*.

Edward's return merely made the atmosphere more tense. Nothing could be guessed from his expression, and neither parent wished to confront the issue. He disappeared upstairs.

"Go and see what he's doing, would you, Axel dear," said Jill.

Returning panting, Axel said, "He is all cover with Salvo."

A puzzled expression, then, "You mean Savlon. God, is he burnt?"

"Ah no, he wipes his cup."

Perplexed again, then, "Ah, you mean Silvo. . . ."

The edginess continued into the next day, and was aided by a sultry closeness in the weather. The sweet smell of the burnt hay still hung in the warm, moist air, so that the incident could never quite be put out of mind.

It was Axel's last day, and Frank stirred himself to liven things up. But it was difficult; the day was quite hot enough for swimming, but the blank sky made the idea of summery entertainment seem uncomfortable and out of place. They sat indoors playing Monopoly, as if it were midwinter. The game was slow and tedious; Frank kept drifting off, then reapplying himself to the state of play with a loud enthusiasm that convinced no one. Axel understood. He kept up pretenses as much for their sake as they did for his, and his eyes shone with forgiveness. And when he left next morning, he and Jill wept in each other's arms, while Frank patted him on the head, looking depressed.

That afternoon a policeman arrived to question Edward about the fire. Edward appeared quite unperturbed by the officer's presence, and flatly denied all guilt. He had been damming a stream in the woods beside the church, he said. If they didn't believe him, they could go and see the dam for themselves. Jill sat anxiously beside him, corroborating what he said as best she could.

"Thank you," said the officer. "We'll leave it there for the moment."

Jill looked tearfully at Edward, but could bring herself to say nothing. Frank wandered into the room and sat drumming his fingers on the glass coffee table. He too looked at his son, saying nothing. He coughed, and shifted his body, as if some distasteful idea were at last forcing its painful passage from thought into speech. Sensing this, Edward rose and left the room, once more deflecting confrontation. Soon they heard him move from room to room upstairs. They looked despondently at one another.

"Back to square one," said Frank.

"I suppose so. I shall miss Axel."

"Me too . . ."

A sound of light feet running down the stairs, and there in the doorway was Edward transformed, all his insouciance given way to an extreme agitation, his eyes moist and his breath coming in short gasps. He looked, Frank thought, as though he was about to confess. But what came whining from Edward's mouth was accusation, not confession: "Axel's stolen my cup."

Frank's arid rain drummed still louder on the table. He heard, as if from a great distance, his wife say, "Haven't you told enough fibs for one day?" and Edward answer plaintively, "It's true," then Jill, "Now don't talk nonsense, dear," and Edward, "Well, it's not in my cupboard and I've searched the whole house for it." Frank perceived so clearly the banality of the ruse. For an instant the perception tugged him equally between anger and pity, but as Edward's whining insistences continued, they began to enter Frank's mind like icy moisture into an overladen cloud. He felt in himself the precipitation, at last, of the nebula of emotions that had been growing in him all summer. Restraints of calm and reason began to fall miraculously away from him, and he sensed the imminence of his complete self-abandonment to the sweet reliefs and releases of blind rage.

Then he felt his hand raising itself to still the room,

and come slamming down on the surface of the coffee table, predicting, as he let it fall, an equal violence of impression should the glass shatter or remain intact.

"That's it," he shouted, the pitch of his voice unnaturally high. "You have thirty seconds to bring back your cup from wherever you've hidden it and apologize for your vile behavior now and for the last six weeks, or I'll thrash you till you wish you'd never been born." Edward was about to insist again, but Frank charged at him, and he fled.

Jill looked startled into her husband's reddening face. "I suppose," she said, "it's possible he has mislaid it."

Trying to restrain his voice, which wanted to bray and whinny like an ass, Frank said, "Don't you see? He's jealous sick of Axel for getting on with us like a normal child, so he thinks up some piece of nonsense to turn us against him. . . . It's the oldest trick in the book."

He looked at his watch. "Right," he shouted. "Where is it, Edward?"

"Ask Axel," came a voice from the top of the stairs.

Frank hurtled out of the room past his wife, and bounded up the stairway after Edward, who ran into his room, slamming the door behind him. Spurring Frank on was the fact, just dawned on him, that the cup had to be handed back to the school at the end of the year, and the thought of all the tedious explanations this would entail if Edward persisted in his obstinacy, which he was quite capable of doing.

He threw open Edward's door, cracking it against the inner wall. Edward was lying face down on the bed, muffling his head in the pillow. An insufficiency, in Frank, of whatever stuff it is that true patriarchs are made of led him to fight with his son as he would with an equal—

tooth and claw—deploying all reserves of strength against the possibility that he might actually lose.

"Give me the damn thing and stop this nonsense," he shouted.

"Axel's got it," came the pillow-gagged reply.

Frank began stomping round the room, turning things over, in a frenzied effort to find the cup, with Edward screaming, "Go away, it isn't here, I haven't got it." Frank grabbed the boy's slender wrist and started shaking him. "Don't lie to me." Edward turned over and started howling. Hot tears were streaming down his face. "Fucker," he bawled, "fucker, fucker, fucker."

"Don't you dare. . . ." Frank started shaking him more violently. Edward's howling took on a hysterical tone; his face was a deep crimson and a high wailing came from his mouth. Frank flung his wrists free. Then he picked up the red cupboard. He turned it door downward and gave it a powerful shake. The door flew open and pebbles, feathers, old china, sea-worn glass, lacy leaves, larks' eggs, Sean, knives—but no silver goblet—all cascaded out and crashed onto the floor. Through his abating rage, Frank became aware that Edward's shrill wail had given way to a mocking, delirious chant: "*Mit. Schlag. Mit. Schlag. Mit. Schlag. Mit. Schlag.*" Frank stared at him, amazed. The ancient, half-solidified double yolks of the smashed rhinoceros egg began to fill the room with the smell of sulfur, and Frank could bear to be there no longer.

"You stay in here without supper till you tell us where the cup is," he said as he shut the door behind him.

He paced up and down the dining room, his limbs trembling, while Jill set the table for supper.

"I know what you're thinking," he said. She made no

reply, and disappeared into the kitchen to fetch the remains of a cold poached salmon and a bowl of oil-
saturated lettuce.

"Trust me," he said. "I know enough about human
nature to know I'm right this time. You'll see." He
tugged loose a flake of salmon, and bolted it down.

They ate their dinner without speaking. "*Mit. Schlag.
Mit. Schlag,*" descended through the house from time
to time, as Edward, with less and less conviction, resumed his chant. Finally they heard nothing but long,
pitiful, uncontrollable cries of grief which continued
long after they had retired, almost as miserable themselves, to their bedroom at the other end of the house.
In the morning, as they breakfasted amid the debris of
last night's supper, the sobs began coursing through the
house again, more subdued than before, but no less depressing to hear.

"Ignore him, ignore him, you'll see . . ." said Frank,
but by lunchtime, as they sat picking desultorily at the
hardening salmon and the wrinkled, clinging lettuce
leaves, the sound was more than Jill could stand.

"I'll go and talk to him."

She was gone a long time. While Frank waited, he
began to imagine that pulling feeling in his chest again.
He savored the potential irony in being killed by a son
who was his not through providence, like most sons, but
through his own choice. He went on to consider that
however modest his own idea of perfection was, and
however forcefully he applied his will to the task of
achieving it, insuperable difficulties always emerged
from nowhere to thwart him. Reaching the limit of his
powers of abstract speculation, he focused once more on
the rose flesh and chain mail of the salmon, and loos-
ened another flake.

Jill came in, holding Edward by the hand. A change
had come over the boy. He was sniffing, pouting slightly,
but his head was hanging as if in shame, and whatever
perversity had possessed him was now most certainly
gone. Jill pushed him gently toward Frank. Seeing
him standing there with his head hung low, his expression frail, exhausted and contrite, Frank realized
at last that things might still turn out all right. He began to feel the sensations of hard-won victory spread
warmly through him, as he listened to Edward's words:
"I threw the cup in the pond. . . . I was jealous of
Axel. . . . I wanted you to be cross with him. . . . I'm
very sorry, and I'll pay for another cup with my pocket
money."

Edward stared at the ground in submissive silence. A
blackbird whistled in the garden, and a light afternoon
breeze rustled through the trellised roses around the
window.

Instincts vindicated, authority acknowledged, father-
hood restored, Frank was magnanimity incarnate. He
forgave, felt certain that a difficult phase in his existence
was now most certainly over, and smiled inwardly at his
earlier reflections on imperfectability. Tedious explanations to the school seemed suddenly a mere trifle.

"You keep your pocket money." He ruffled Edward's
hair. He would present the school with a bigger, better
cup, "The Frank Fowler Award for Achievement on the
Pitch." It had a ring to it.

From that day forth, Edward was a reformed character. The incident seemed to have adjusted the constella-
tion of his personality, so that he was able suddenly to
master the trick, which had so long eluded him, of being
good. And he devoted himself to goodness with a con-
vert's zeal. The objects fallen from his red cupboard

were slung out like discredited idols. Tantrum energy
was channeled into deeds of filial obeisance. He laid and
cleared the table each mealtime, with such reverence
that he might have been performing some sacred ritual.
He contrived ways of being good with all the craft and
ingenuity he had once applied to his intransigence.
Frank and Jill's tennis shoes would be freshly whitened
by a mysterious hand on mornings of local tournaments;
jars filled with flowers would appear in their bedroom,
the glass panes of the gas lamp were cleaned and polished to a brilliant clarity. . . .

The policeman came again. Edward admitted partial
blame for starting the fire, but in his confession named
the Davis children as the instigators of the crime.

"They led you on, so to speak," said the policeman.

"That's right," said Edward.

"Well, don't let it happen again."

Colin and Jim Davis were taken into care. Beverley
and her parents moved out of the village. Jill found herself nervously watching Edward for signs of remorse.
She was unsure whether her nervousness was in case he
did feel remorse, or in case he felt none at all. He seemed
unmoved, and she, catching herself daydreaming about
having to account for something unspecified to someone, began wondering uneasily exactly what was this
prodigy she and Frank had created. "I must be mad to
complain, though," she told herself, thinking how perfectly this creation corresponded to the child she and
Frank had once imagined having. But watching him on
the court one day, playing eager ballboy to Frank and a
neighbor, she felt an irresistible urge to probe, to see
how far down into the old Edward this angelic surface
reached.

That evening, as they sat together on the white leather

sofa watching television, she said, looking at the screen, "Don't you miss Beverley?"

Frank looked at her angrily. "Now that's all behind us," he said. "Let's let bygones be bygones, shall we—eh, Edward?" He patted his son affectionately on the knee.

But Edward wanted to reply. "No, I don't miss her. If I'd been the judge I'd have sent her into care along with her brothers." Edward spoke in the peculiarly pure, self-possessed tone he had adopted after the incident with the cup. A faint smile came to his lips. He slid off the sofa and turned off the television. He stood up stiffly, still smiling his faint smile. Looking toward his parents, he said in that high, pure voice: "Beverley Davis, I sentence you to ten million years' hard labor for committing foul and wicked crimes with your villainous brothers, and even worse, for plotting to lead astray the wonderfully good and brilliant Edward Fowler, a pillar of our society and England's finest ballboy."

He broke into peals of high laughter and fell back onto the sofa. Frank too was chuckling with delight. He beamed triumphantly at Jill, as if he had just proved some point beyond all possible dispute. Jill hesitantly joined in the laughter, then bit her lip, and felt more like crying. But after all, what was there to cry about? Through the bottle-glass window she could see the blurred globe of light from the gas lamp, floating beside the house like a charm against all evil. "So relax," she told herself. "This is what you wanted."

The following spring, Axel's father came to England on business. He called on the Fowlers late one afternoon for tea. A fine rain came and went in sprays crisply against the window, and the spring wind frisked through the bright new leaves on the chestnut trees. Jill had not seen Werner since the day he had married her cousin and barely recognized this tall, smiling man as he kissed her full on the lips. Frank had never met him at all. The two men were of an age where they couldn't but wonder what the other had been doing in the war, but each made efforts to look as though nothing could be further from his thoughts. They had not progressed beyond formalities, when Edward came in from his first day back at school. He said he had been made head of his class, and began to describe an elaborate system of informing that he had already established. He seemed hardly to register who Werner was, and showed no flicker of interest when Axel's name was mentioned.

"And how *is* Axel?" asked Jill.

"Oh, Axel, he's well, you know. Growing into a fine young man, like Edward here. I could wish him a little more . . . athletic, you know. He has too much his mother's build, I think"—he grinned at Jill—"but you can't have everything, can you? And he tries hard to please his old father." He chuckled and put his hands behind his head. "We were so proud of him, you know, when he came back from England with that cup for winning in your village sports. It was really so . . ." But the rest of Werner's words were lost on Frank and Jill. They stared at their son in uncomprehending silence while sprays of rain crackled against the windows. Jill felt as if something sharp and heavy, like a metal door, had banged down inside her, and up into Frank's mouth came a phlegm that tasted horribly like the smell of pig manure. They stared at their son, but Edward . . . Edward looked through them with his cool blue eyes, as if he had heard nothing, as if he were beyond recall, in orbit upon another planet, where the voices from this one could no longer reach him.

The Spoiling

W HEN RONALD'S WIFE left him, it was understood
that the Boyce family flag would go on flying under
his name. The friends they had appropriated during the
ten years of their deteriorating marriage would, with the
two children, the Volvo, and the large Kensington
house, remain his property. Margaret, it was understood, would take herself altogether elsewhere to find an
altogether new life. It was, after all, she who had wanted
to bring an end to the business and, as Ronald reasoned
in his special aggrieved-but-magnanimous voice, it was
the least she could do to refrain from disrupting the
children's upbringing by removing them from the home
which had nurtured their healthy little bodies and minds
with such abundance of love and prosperity.

From the start, Ronald had established himself as dic-
tator of furnishings and family customs in the Boyce
household. He had a natural instinct for covering and
softening—quince fitted carpeting throughout, lilac
wallpaper covering every wall but those of the still-bare
hallway, a large and undistinguished collection of hunt-
ing and sporting prints covering the wallpaper in the
dining room, and, to his wife's perpetual embarrassment, a series of photographs of her as a naked toddler
on Brighton beach, which Ronald had insisted on fram-
ing and hanging in a column beside the walnut cabinet

133

in the drawing room. Later on, he added pictures of his own children in similar circumstances and, finally, one of himself being presented to the Queen Mother at the opening ceremony of the company's new factory. Curiously, perhaps, he did not remove the pictures of his wife when she left him, and they hang there still, the first things to meet the eyes of the guests as they arrive at this, the eleventh of his annual New Year's Eve buffet parties.

The guests are a mixture. There are the business fraternity and their wives; these are the good solid friends who were so supportive when Ronald's wife left him: the managing director and his wife, who are affable and fuss over the children, forever telling them what a clever man their daddy is, and how he will soon be on the board; Colin Porter, the firm accountant—a bachelor who takes himself rather seriously but, as Ronald has discovered, quite likes to be patronized; Gordon Cavendish, Bob Goldsmith, who now works for a rival company, Teddy Bantock—all good solid men with good solid wives. Then there is the motley collection of guests employed variously in or around the fringes of "Art." Ronald is doubly proud of this collection—first, as novelties from the world of culture, to be paraded in front of his business colleagues, and second, because they were originally friends of his wife's and their presence here today both indicates a highly gratifying transference of affections and reconfirms his sense of his own righteousness.

The doorbell rings with increasing frequency. Ronald likes to make warm physical contact with each guest as he or she arrives; handshakes and backpatting for the men, kisses and hugs for the women. He has learned the importance of the bold gesture—that most people will accept for real any posture you care to present them with, and that while he might be tortured in private by a nagging sense of his own littleness, the world is prepared to accept him at face value, as a man who has suffered nobly and attained a certain grandeur. He is entitled to whatever intimacy he can extract. And indeed, in the faces of the guests as they enter, he discerns nothing but mute expressions of admiration and sympathy; mute, that is, until the rather brash Bella Suzman, who makes customized quilts, bursts in, flings her arms around Ronald, holds him away for a minute, gazing mournfully into his eyes, and then declaims her opening speech: "Ronnie, you are marvelous, after all you've been through. How you have the guts and determination to soldier on as if nothing has happened, when we all know how difficult it must have been for you" (here she pauses for breath), "I simply cannot understand. And the children . . ." (here she trails off).

Ronald's head is tilted in humility, a resigned smile fixed on his handsome face: "You're always so kind, Bella —let me take your coat" (peeling the fur from her back). "I'm very philosophic about it all now. Besides" (laughing), "your quilt was never quite big enough for the two of us, so perhaps it's just as well." He places a glass of champagne in her hand, casts his eye over the room, which has begun to fill up, sees Colin Porter, the firm accountant, standing alone feigning interest in the design of his glass, and, ever the good host, takes Bella across the room to meet him. "Colin, meet my old friend Bella. Bella's a designer . . . Colin's our resident financial wizard, aren't you, Colin old chap?"

There is something edgy in Ronald's style tonight, something a little off-balance—the condescension toward Colin is not tempered with quite the usual warmth. However, Colin does not register this, and as Ronald drifts gracefully away from the pair, he catches the sound of Colin's monotone: "Well, I wouldn't say wizard. . . ."

The room is alive with the sound of well-heeled Londoners engaging in conversation. The Christmas tree is still there, decorated with the usual Czechoslovakian glass baubles, and the picture frames are all hung with pieces of tinsel. The central heating is perhaps a little too high, though at the moment it is giving the guests that glow of protective comfort so conducive to an easy flow of chatter.

The bell rings. It can only be one person; the others have all arrived. Ronald glides through the guests, turns deftly into the hall, prepares a solemn smile, and opens the door.

"Hilary, welcome, come in. And you've brought Marty too, good."

He does not kiss Hilary, but he pats Marty on the head.

"Hello, Ronald. I'm so sorry we're late, but Marty needed some persuading—didn't you, dear?—and I couldn't leave him on his own."

"I should think not," says Ronald, patting Marty again. "He can help Lizzie and Robert pass round the dips and things if he likes—would you like to do that, Marty?"

The boy stares up at Ronald through the thick lenses of a pair of round tortoiseshell glasses. His fair hair hangs lifelessly down the white cheeks of his expressionless face. He blinks and mutters, "I don't mind."

Hilary, thirty-seven, tired-looking, pointed but not unattractive features, a fractional nervousness in her movements, does not seem the kind of woman to cause Ronald much anxiety. And were it not for the particular nature of her circumstances, in relation to those of Ronald, there might indeed be no cause for this embarrassed fidgetiness that seems to be afflicting both of them as they enter the drawing room.

She was the best friend of Margaret—Ronald's ex-wife —since their days together at art school. Margaret, honoring the unspoken agreement with her husband to the last detail, or perhaps from a genuine desire for a complete break, visited Hilary for the last time six months ago, and made it clear that she would not be in touch again. The bewildered Hilary took the news as merely another phase in the bad dream which had begun with her own husband's incipient alcoholism, and had become a nightmare with his death two years ago in a journalists' bar in Hanoi.

Since then Hilary has lived alone with her son in a flat in Stockwell. She has a part-time administrative job on the paper that used to employ her husband, and earns barely enough to support herself and Marty. The years have accustomed her to a life occupied, for the most part, with the business of simply keeping things going, but they have not dulled in her any hope of a more comfortable kind of existence. She makes no attempt to conceal from herself the fact that, while she is able to cope on her own, a man who could support her as her husband once supported her would make life very much more tolerable. Such a man might also relieve the unhealthy closeness with her son which she has found herself being wedged into.

She is not unaware that mutual friends were plotting a match between herself and Ronald long before he and his wife finally divorced. Neither is she unaware that Ronald is attracted to her. The assiduous attention he began paying her when her husband started to collapse, the use of her bereavement as a license to soft-talk her and to peer more than merely sympathetically into her eyes, never escaped her. She was not exactly flattered, because there was something not exactly wholesome in Ronald's manner of flattery. But there was a shrewd aspect to her otherwise quite ingenuous personality, which told her that, when all was said and done, Ronald was a good deal better than nothing; that in many ways he was in fact remarkably suitable.

Yet she never encouraged him. At first she hung back because the whole business of affairs with married men was too alien to the life she was brought up to for it to occur to her as a real possibility. But even afterward, when there was no question of deception on either side, and his desire for her was plain for all to see, there was still something about Ronald which made the prospect of intimacy with him seem slightly repulsive.

The title "best friend" became purely nominal after Margaret married Ronald, but Hilary was still able to witness the breakdown of that marriage—and the transformation of Margaret from a cheerful and talented young woman into the bitter wife who seemed to delight in embarrassing and humiliating her husband at every available opportunity—from a rather closer point of view than anybody else. And what she saw did not quite support the theory in general circulation, that Margaret had wanted to be an artist, but through a failure of nerve had decided to marry young and raise a family instead, visiting the consequences of her frustration upon her patient husband. Hilary saw that things were by no means as simple as this, nor as one-sided. She had once called round on the couple, to be met with a frosty greeting from Ronald, and the sight of Margaret crumpled up on the sofa nursing a swollen lip and a bruised chin.

Years later, Margaret used to hint that she had given up painting because Ronald, jealous at the prospect of a wife who might become more successful than himself, had poured such incessant scorn on her efforts that her confidence had been shattered. However, by this time Margaret was so obviously soured by her marriage that Hilary could not quite believe what she said, or hinted at. Besides, she suspected that Margaret might be jealous of her, or at least determined that the man whom she was going to leave should not find happiness in another woman with any ease, especially when the other woman was supposed to be her own best friend. So while Hilary took great pains to show Margaret that she was innocent of any complicity with Ronald, she kept an open mind on the question of Ronald's real nature.

Apart from the satisfaction to be had from seducing his wife's best friend, Ronald has a perfectly practical reason for wishing to wed Hilary: he finds life as a single parent uncomfortable and lonely. Of course, he adores his two children, but a nine-year-old daughter and an eight-year-old son are more trouble than company, and a succession of helps have come and gone with an alarming rapidity.

Witnessing Hilary's self-sacrificing devotion to her sick husband gave Ronald ample proof of her wifely virtues —sufficient, indeed, for him to have conceived what he believes to be a real, passionate affection for her. He has designed the occasion tonight as a showcase for the kind of life he has to offer Hilary: a life full of warmth, hospitality, geniality, stimulating conversation, good food, limitless hot water—in short, everything a reasonable woman could ask for. And Hilary, too, knows as she walks into the warm, crowded room that tonight may be a night for certain decisions.

Ronald summons his children—"Lizzie, Robert, come here."

They come over, their little hands bearing dishes of crisps and Twiglets. Lizzie, the elder child, has pretty but oddly unchildlike features, as if her face has reached adulthood before her body. And standing in her quaint, old-fashioned green velvet dress with frills around the collar and wrists, a look of extreme alertness in her eyes, she makes a strong contrast of independent individuality to her brother, who, from all appearances, could still be any little boy.

"Marty is going to help you pass the things around, but take him to the kitchen first, and give him some orange juice."

They have met Marty before, so the extreme unwill- ingness to meet others of their kind that afflicts most children is somewhat alleviated. Nevertheless, they have not reached the age when one's natural hostility to strangers, or near strangers, is automatically concealed, and the looks they give Marty are not friendly. Marty is unwilling to leave his mother's side, but he does not wish to appear timid. He sullenly follows the other two into the kitchen, squirming out of the way of a final pat from Ronald as he does so.

In the center of the large, tile-floored, Formica- surfaced kitchen stand two tables on which are arranged the plates and cutlery, and the various dishes to be con- sumed later tonight. A single lamp in a conical shade, suspended from the ceiling directly above the tables, is all that illuminates the room at the moment. It gives off a bright, but very localized, beam, highlighting the ta- bles but leaving the rest of the room quite dim. The effect is to intensify the various colors of the food to a dramatic pitch, and so to give the whole spread an ethereal quality, as if it were a glossy photograph from the food pages of a women's magazine, enlarged and made three-dimensional. For a moment, Marty is transfixed by the sight of the dishes as they glisten from the tables. On one table are the savories. Bowls of pink taramasalata, yogurt and cucumber salad, a pale green avocado mousse, rice salad, olives, sliced tomatoes, and half eggs stuffed with a mixture of their own yolks, mayonnaise, and red cayenne pepper are arranged next to two large flat dishes, one containing translucent slices of Parma ham, and the other, slices of cold roast beef graded from, at one end, a well-cooked gray-brown to, at the other end, a rare blood-red. And finally, there are two huge earthenware bowls, one of potato salad in a rich-looking mayonnaise dressing, its goldness set off by green flecks of chopped chives, and the other of pieces of cold chicken cooked in tarragon, cream, cherries, and burnt almonds. On the second table are the cheeses and desserts—two more bowls, one containing a fresh fruit salad and the other a creamy chocolate-glazed mound of profiteroles.

Marty acquired, with his father's encouragement, a sophisticated palate at an early age. In fact, it was due largely to the promise of such delicacies as he now beholds that his mother was able to persuade him to come tonight. And he is clearly not disappointed, although a habit of reserve limits his reaction toward what he now sees to a long, expressionless stare. Despite this reserve, Robert quickly perceives that Marty is impressed with the food; he stands in front of Marty, picks up a profiterole, and pops it into his mouth, looking provocatively at Marty as he does so, as if to dare him to take one too. But before an impulse to take up the challenge can even begin to shape itself, Lizzie smacks her little brother on the hand. "I'm telling Daddy you took one of those," she says smartly.

The boy's face puckers up in fury. "*You* took one before," he says, his high voice full of reproach.

"That's because Daddy said I could for helping."

"Well, I've helped too."

She ignores this remark and asks Marty if he would like some orange juice.

"No, thanks," is his muttered reply.

Robert breaks into a fit of laughter, half put-on, half genuine, and dances around the table, singing, "He doesn't want your orange juice, he doesn't want your orange juice," over and over until his sister smacks him sharply on the arm. This time the puckering face looks dangerously close to tears. Sensing trouble, Lizzie quickly pops another profiterole into her brother's mouth in an attempt to pacify him, and then, with an instinct for sisterliness, takes one herself. For an instant, the boy stands still, uncertain which emotion to give way to—tearful anger or conspiratorial glee. To the relief of his sister, he decides on the latter.

"Now *you* have one," he says to Marty, holding another out to him.

"No, thanks," says Marty again. He is not merely being unsociable; the fact is that he does not have an ordinary child's sweet tooth, and the thought of a sticky ball of chocolate, chou pastry, and whipped cream does not particularly appeal to him. What he would accept, and what he is longing to be offered, is something from the other table—something with the savory taste of *real* food. But no offer is made.

"Well, I'll just have to eat it myself then," says Robert, putting it into his mouth and turning to his sister with a slightly uncertain smile. She does not smile back.

The key to the power she exerts over her younger brother is her unpredictability. Her seemingly irrational swings between sweet indulgence and high-handed intolerance have successfully baffled him into crediting her with the mysterious motives of a superior creature. He chews nervously on his profiterole, awaiting the unfolding of the significance of her cold expression.

"This time I really am telling Daddy," she says, and walks toward the door.

Robert catches her by the waist of her dress; there is a tearing sound, though no visible damage is done. She screams with anger and begins clawing at his arm to free herself—"Let go, you stupid idiot!"—but the boy's fear of being informed on lends him a tenaciousness which she cannot break. However, while he clings dumbly to her, his head and arms buried in the folds about her waist, she coolly assesses the situation, looks about for a weapon, sees a wooden spoon on the shelf by her, grabs it, and briefly catching the eye of Marty, who is looking on forlornly, brings it down on her brother's head. Robert howls, and lets go instantly. Now it is his turn to try and seek refuge in a parent; he makes for the door, but Lizzie is standing in front of it, brandishing her wooden spoon.

"You can stop being a crybaby," she tells him. "Anyway, it serves you right for tearing my dress."

Robert's howls melt into whimpers of self-pity. He slumps down on a chair, nursing his bruised head.

"You wouldn't have done that if Mummy was here," he sobs.

"Well, she isn't here, is she?"

"Where is your mother?" asks Marty. The other children are startled at his sudden intrusion into their private quarrel; they stare at him a moment before Lizzie replies, "She's gone away."

"Why?" asks Marty.

Before Lizzie can answer, Robert interrupts sulkily, "Daddy sent her away."

"Oh, Robert! Don't tell lies!" says his sister, shocked.

"It's true. He sent her away because she was bad and made him cross, and if she was here now she'd punish you."

"No she wouldn't. Daddy wouldn't let her. You know what he did last time she punished me."

There is a pause.

"What did he do?" asks Marty, his curiosity aroused.

"He smacked her," says Lizzie, with smug simplicity, to which Robert adds with venom: "He hit her on the face till she bled and the next day her eye was all purple and puffed up."

"He hit her?" Marty asks.

"She was bad and he said if it wasn't for her always saying and doing the wrong thing he'd have been on the board years ago, and now she's gone, he'll probably be on the board very soon," says Robert, hesitating a moment before he adds, "Doesn't your father ever hit your mother?"

Lizzie stares at her brother, appalled; their father specifically warned them to make no mention of Marty's father, but the tactless question has been asked, and hangs unanswered for a moment in the silence of the dim room.

"My father's dead."

There is no audible emotion in Marty's voice, but Robert knows he has blundered into something beyond his comprehension. He looks helplessly from Marty to his sister, as if to ask for her support. But she looks at him blankly, unwilling to be conscripted to his aid or perhaps simply as dumbstruck as himself. By a kind of crude, guileless logic, Robert's mind turns to the profiteroles again. He takes one out of the bowl and offers it to Marty. "Go on, nobody'll notice."

A glance at his sister tells him that she does not disapprove of this stratagem. Again, Marty refuses.

"Why not? Don't you like them?" asks Robert.

"No, not really." Then, feeling he has somehow earned a privilege by virtue of having been asked the indelicate question about his dead father, Marty adds: "But can we have some of the other stuff, from the other table?"

The two children stare at him blankly. The thought of taking what they think of as adult food, to be consumed only at meals, has never entered their minds. It is not part of their game, and they are plainly at a loss to see why anybody could possibly want to take a slice of cold ham when they weren't supposed to.

"No, you can't do that," says Lizzie coolly.

But Marty needs to hear no words to know that he has transgressed in some small but fatal way; that any foothold he had made in the entrance to the private world of these children has been abruptly lost. And with an only child's hypersensitivity to the intricacies of other children's affections, he senses a feeling, long familiar to him, of being gently, but irredeemably, cast out.

The process of mutual withdrawing is undelayed; Marty relapses from his brief talkativeness back into sullen silence, and the other two, no longer interested in him, drift out of the room bearing replenished dishes of crisps, closing the door a little behind them.

Marty lingers in the room, feeling an uncomfortable mood of directionless resentment descending upon him.

He gazes at the table of savories, hesitating for a moment. Then, pursing his lips, he reaches forward, takes a stuffed egg, and crams it, whole, into his mouth. It tastes good. As he chews it he remembers a time, three years ago, when his father, in one of the moods of complete benevolence that came to him less and less frequently as he approached his end, took him to a Greek restaurant in Soho. He filled Marty with delicacies from a table of hors d'oeuvres, till he could eat no more, all the time giving him little sips of wine so that the warm glow of the room seemed subsumed within his own temples. He finds it difficult to think of his father—such efforts as he makes to summon up the memory of the dead man are met, more often than not, with blankness. He was aware of a general sigh of relief breathed by the friends and relatives when his father died, but he knew that for his mother, the relief nowhere near compensated for the loss, and whether by virtue of his constant closeness with his mother, or some real, deep-rooted affection for the man, the feelings of the mother became the feelings of the son. So while he finds it difficult to recreate the image of his father, he returns to the task again and again, struggling for the satisfaction of an occasional fleeting vision of the heavy, bearded man hunched over a typewriter that seemed ridiculously small beneath his large hands.

But now he cannot make the vision come. His concentration is diverted by something which has been vaguely hovering behind his thoughts all evening; something which began as an unaccountable sense of unease on seeing the tense formality of Ronald's greeting of his mother, and which was silently shaping itself into a distinct, attributable emotion during the scene, just passed, with Lizzie and Robert. It is a sense of why he and his

mother are here tonight, and now, as the demands of
this sense to come into the foreground of his mind force
the small, pale boy to abandon his efforts to summon his
father's specter, Marty feels himself overwhelmed by the
sudden and fearful awareness that he is going to have
Ronald for a father, and Lizzie and Robert for brother
and sister. In contrast to his mother's soul-searching hes-
itancy about this union, Marty's attitude to it comes with
the utter clarity of unswerving instinct, and the instinct
tells him very simply "no." But the certainty of this reaction brings with it only another, more painful sense;
that of his complete powerlessness to avert the imposi-
tion of family bonds with people for whom he has less
than no affection. With the feeling of panic that attends
the knowledge that one is unavoidably going to be made
unhappy, Marty quits the room, in search of his mother.

As he opens the living room door he is met by a rush
of heat which, if momentarily pleasant, quickly becomes
uncomfortable. The guests are still standing, but are
showing signs of weakening under the excessive warmth.
Handkerchiefs are being wiped across moist foreheads,
layers of clothing discarded, hands stretched out to convenient ledges for support. There are too many people
for the hum of conversation ever to fade entirely, but as
Marty looks about for his mother, he notices how,
among some of the groups of adults, poised as if in earnest conversation with each other, for all the shifts of
facial expression and all the throat-clearing, nothing is
actually said for long moments, until the phantom of
silence that hovers over them flickers on to the next
group.

Marty does not immediately see his mother. He peers
about, but the moist heat of the room mists up the lenses
of his glasses—cool from the unheated kitchen. He takes

them off to wipe them. At once all edges lose their clarity; the people in the room blur into indistinct figures, remote and meaningless, their physical presence reduced for a moment to the same level of vague irrelevance to the certainties of Marty's world as that of their motley individualities. As he polishes the lenses, certain rearrangements of grouping occur in the room so that, on his replacing the glasses, among the figures that shift back into focus are those of his mother and Ronald standing close together in the far left-hand corner, apparently rapt in conversation. He moves toward them, bluntly ignoring the well-intentioned smiles beamed down upon him by the guests through whom he weaves. But he hesitates before interrupting the couple. They do not appear to notice him, although Marty knows he is standing directly in Ronald's line of vision. He wonders whether perhaps he ought not to intrude, but the idea that he could possibly be in a position wherein approaching his mother would amount to "intrusion" only increases his anxiety. And so, abandoning all scruples, he steps forward and gives his mother's sleeve a sharp tug.

For a moment she does not respond, and Ronald, taking no notice of the boy, continues to talk to her in a low, serious tone. Marty gives the sleeve another, sharper tug, his desire for attention growing in proportion to his sense of being ignored. This time his mother places her free hand on his, in a gesture of vague reassurance. But Marty needs more than this. He tugs the sleeve again and says in a voice shrill with angry impatience, "Mum, look at me."

She looks down at her son with an abstracted smile.

"What is it, dear?" she asks, but in a tone that does not express much concern, and her son, feeling rebuffed, makes no answer. Seeing that Hilary has acknowledged

Marty, Ronald does so too and, in a voice that is intended to be jolly, asks him why he isn't helping Lizzie and Robert with the crisps. Before Marty can reply, Hilary adds, with an insensitivity that is unusual for her, "Yes, dear, do go and help the other two. Ronald and I are having a talk."

Marty is visibly shocked by this apparent callousness. That his mother and Ronald are not "talking" but "having a talk" confirms his dismayed sense of things going hugely awry. He turns away from the pair and wanders aimlessly among the guests, his only care being to avoid the glance of Bella Suzman, who, he fears, is rooting to make a fuss over him. There is a growing lassitude in the room; it is getting late, and the guests are impatient to eat. Ronald, normally so attentive at these functions, has, for the last fifteen or twenty minutes, neglected to fill the empty glasses, or to reshuffle the guests, so that a slight sense of premature staleness seems to have descended on the company. Lizzie and Robert have retired, bored, to an upstairs bedroom. The plates of crisps they are supposed to be passing around are lying abandoned on the walnut cabinet.

Marty finds himself in front of this cabinet, and notices the photographs of the Boyce family aligned above it. He gazes sulkily at the gilt-framed pictures, automatically filling and refilling his mouth with crisps as he does so. He recognizes the figure of Ronald, his hair slicked back, standing stiffly in a row with other smartly dressed young men all smiling proudly, in the picture with the Queen Mother. The picture irritates Marty; he needs to know nothing of its circumstances to understand that it speaks of exactly the same kind of worthless, fawning pride that he has seen and despised in boys at his school. He passes on to the pictures of naked toddlers playing on the beach. Two of the children he recognizes as Lizzie and Robert. They are shown in a very cute sequence of five photographs in which Lizzie appears to be teasing Robert by holding an apple just beyond his reach. The little boy's face gets crosser and crosser in each picture, until the final one, where he is sitting on the sand weeping, oblivious of the arm that Lizzie is extending—this time, Marty guesses, offering him the apple in all earnest.

There are some more photographs, of a child whom Marty does not recognize. It is a little girl standing, sitting, and running on the beach. In one of the pictures, her face is animated by a look of intense delight that captivates Marty, as it has captivated everyone who has looked at it. Marty wonders whether the girl might be a third Boyce child who perhaps died of some fatal illness and was never spoken of since. But something about the photograph—its slightly faded appearance, and the air of its subject—suggests to him that it is of another age.

He wanders away, reaching no conclusion about the picture. The crisps have dried out his mouth, and the cigarette smoke in the hot room is furring up his tongue with an unpleasant taste. He heads toward the kitchen with the vague intention of getting a drink of water. However, before he reaches the door, his attention is caught by an untouched glass of champagne standing on a ledge beside the Christmas tree. A momentary qualm is swiftly disposed of—Marty is strictly forbidden to drink alcohol, but this merely enhances the delight of its effects. So, slipping behind the Christmas tree, the glass of champagne in his hand, Marty proceeds to sip the drink steadily down.

It is flat, but it rises to his head no less quickly because of that, and well before he finishes it, he feels its effects

beginning to work on him. Through the branches of the
tree, the room seems more detached from him than
ever. A man, standing alone in the center of the room,
is looking toward the Christmas tree. He does not notice
Marty until the boy jogs one of the branches while lifting
the glass to his lips. The man looks startled. It is Colin
Porter, the firm accountant, long ago deserted by Bella
Suzman. He moves toward the tree, but suddenly checks
himself, and turns away to hover on the edge of a group
of guests making listless small talk on the other side of
the room. Marty derives an impish satisfaction from the
power he apparently has to deflect would-be approach-
ers. He feels safe behind the Christmas tree, and stands
for a while, gazing intently at the colored glass baubles,
until they seem to radiate light, and not merely reflect it.
Then he looks dreamily back into the room, the after-
images of the baubles floating before his eyes to mingle
with the faces of the guests. But any sense of well-being
that may be settling upon him is abruptly punctured;
there have been more movements in the room, and once
again the figures of his mother and Ronald are visible to
Marty. They seem more rapt than ever now. Ronald is
saying something to Hilary in a low voice. Marty can tell
it is a low voice, because his mother is evidently straining
to hear. She has a very serious expression on her face.
At one moment she looks toward the Christmas tree. It
seems to Marty that she must be able to see him through
the branches, and he stares back, but she turns away
again, without having registered him.

   Marty looks at the pair, Ronald still talking intently,
his mother listening in silence, a slight unease in her
expression. The champagne has numbed Marty's sense
of angered injury, but has not dispersed it. He wonders
what Ronald is saying, but already knows in his heart

that it is part of a process which will somehow separate him from his mother, and which he is helpless to prevent. He studies Ronald closely, and the more he watches him, the more he finds the man's bearing and manner repellent. Everything about him carries a look of duplicity, his features seem as if contorted into pleasantness from a natural set of belligerence. One hand is tucked within the breast of his jacket, the other toys with an empty glass, as if to denote relaxation. His head is deferentially bowed to Hilary, and he stands unusually close to her, assuming the intimacy of an old friendship.

Marty tips the last drops of champagne down his throat, and moves out from behind the Christmas tree. He has had enough of this party and wants to go home. The certainty that he will have to stay to the end fills him with a sudden willful petulance. If he is to be forced to endure an evening which seems to have been designed to make him miserable, then at least he can be spared the necessity of accommodating himself to those present. Bella Suzman confronts him with a huge grin, and is about to talk to him, but he shoves rudely past her, and walks out of the room before she can utter.

He stands in the cool quiet of the inner hall, wondering what to do. The large mirror throws back a reflection of him looking unnaturally white. He gazes at himself until the image blurs around its edges and seems almost to dissolve. It is a fancy he has, that certain select people have the power to transform matter, and that he is being taught the secrets of the process, prior to being initiated into this mysterious elite. It is always with slight trepidation that he tries to stare his own reflection into oblivion, the fear that he will undergo some terrifying metamorphosis contending with his rational skepticism about the whole business. A noise from the top of the staircase interrupts his efforts. He looks up and sees in the gloom Robert's face protruding between two of the banister railings on the second flight of stairs. The two boys look at each other in silence for a moment, then Robert's head recedes into the shadows and Marty hears him scuffling off.

Having left the drawing room, Marty is loath to reenter it. But he must occupy himself somehow. He walks up and down the hallway, rapping his knuckles sharply on the radiator casing until the strange mixture of petulance and anxiety that possesses him begins to make the glaring whiteness of the hall, unrelieved except by the mirror reflecting only the doorway opposite, unbearable in its monotony. He walks along the corridor, toward the back of the house. There is a door on the right, beyond the back of the drawing room, which he guesses must be a second entrance into the kitchen. He opens it and walks in. There on the table, beneath the muted arc of the suspended lamp, the evening's food still stands, the contents of each bowl and dish glowing with its pristine color. Marty is drawn irresistibly toward it. In the hush of the room, and to the boy still half drunk from his glassful of champagne, the food has all the power of attraction that an open coffer of Inca gold and jewels might have for the first traveler to penetrate its secret vault. And it is with something of the guilty delight of such a traveler that Marty begins to consume his treasure.

His intention, at first, is just to have a little taste; he will limit himself to one item, or perhaps two. The question is which two? After a moment's deliberation he settles on the beef and the potato salad. He selects a slice of beef from the bloodiest end of the dishful, and pushes it, whole, into his mouth. As he chews it, savoring the juice imparted from its fibers, he dips two fingers into the bowl of potato salad, and scoops out a big yellow mound of the stuff, which, after he has swallowed the beef, he promptly crams into his mouth.

That dispensed with, and the taste of raw beef and mayonnaise lingering so pleasantly on his tongue, it occurs to Marty that nobody will know the difference if he has just a little taste of everything. Accordingly, he begins a gastronomic tour of the whole table. First he dips his fingers into the taramasalata, delighting in its fishy, oily essence. Then he broaches the yogurt and cucumber salad, finding it a little dull in comparison, so that he has to return for another taste of the taramasalata to restore that original delight. Next, in quick succession, a slice of dressed tomato, another stuffed egg, a fingerful of the delicate avocado mousse, the largest slice of ham, and the flesh of a green olive the size of a plum, all disappear down his throat. He pauses a moment to allow the mingled flavors time to release their aromas fully in his mouth. His enjoyment is marred a little by the anguish that still nags at him and by a faint feeling of nausea that always follows when he drinks alcohol. But he concentrates on his business all the more purposefully, in an effort to dispel these distractions. He deems the rice salad too plain to be worth bothering with, so that all that remains for his attention is the bowl of cold chicken.

This poses a slight moral problem for Marty: the pieces of chicken are a little too large for his conscience to turn a blind eye to; moreover, they will produce evidence, in the form of gnawed bones, which will need to be removed. He tentatively dips a finger into the bowl, and tastes the sauce. The combination of cream, tarragon, black cherries, and burnt almonds is altogether new to him, and its light, sweet freshness holds him, for a second, in utter possession. All his scruples about taking the chicken vanish immediately, and selecting a piece of breast and wing, he proceeds to tear at the soft white meat, until there is nothing left but sinew and bones. These he places on the table, next to the olive stone, meaning to dispose of them in a minute.

First, however, he must have something more to drink. There are some uncorked bottles of what looks like red wine on the sideboard by the washing machine. Marty steps over, and picks one up. He takes a mouthful straight from the bottle, swallows half of it, but as the bitter flavor of retsina registers on his tongue, he is suddenly incapable of swallowing the rest, and in a spasm of disgust, he spits it out. He looks in horror at the splattered red stain at his feet, but the desire to clear his mouth of the taste presses more urgently than the problem of clearing up the mess. He swills out his mouth with water, but the bitterness will not wash away. He returns to the table, thinking that the taste of something stronger than the wine might do the trick. A large scoop of taramasalata seems to make things better. But to make sure, Marty helps himself to another slice of ham, and very quickly finds himself unable to resist making another tour of the table.

He is vaguely aware of somebody moving about in the next-door room, the dining room, which leads in turn to the drawing room. But while he senses danger, he is too deeply engaged in his private orgy to retreat. There is something a little manic, this time, about the way in which Marty picks from dish to dish. The way he thrusts his hands into the food and back into his mouth seems exaggerated, as if he is investing each gesture with some passionate and private significance—and this suggestion

is strengthened by the fact that he is muttering something as he eats. The actual words are unintelligible, lost
in the grunts and gulps with which he consumes the
food, but their tone is unmistakably malevolent. In fact,
most of the muttering does not consist of words at all;
Marty is losing himself in a private fantasy of denuncia-
tion against Ronald and his children, and the sounds he
is making are, on the whole, no more than a kind of
musical accompaniment to his mental maledictions.
And these, too, have no articulate shape; the growing
violence of the boy's reaction against his host has dis-
tilled itself into an antipathy that is too pure to need
words for its expression.

The door from the dining room opens.

Marty, his back to the door, and his concentration
completely absorbed in wrapping a piece of avocado-
mousse-coated beef around a chicken drumstick, does
not hear the click of the handle. But he does hear, a
moment later, a shocked voice cry out, "Jesus Christ!"
as Ronald takes in the sound and sight of the small boy
muttering, and stooped over a buffet table covered in
the debris of bones, olive stones, pieces of fat, half-eaten
eggs, and unidentifiable blobs of dropped or discarded
food.

Marty swings around and stares, terrified, into Ronald's face. But this face, unlike the face of Robert between the banister railings, does not disappear when
stared at. Instead it advances slowly toward Marty, fixing
the boy's eyes with an expression of hopeless anger.
Marty backs off to the other side of the table. The man
approaches. He is breathing heavily. His eyes move
slowly back and forth between the ruined feast and the
culprit cowering on the other side of the table. And
Marty gazes back in appalled fascination at this meta-

morphosed version of the suave Ronald from the drawing room. Gazes at him, held to the table as if cornered,
not by any physical boundary, but by the enthralled terror a victim has for its predator. Suddenly some tensile
string, which seems to hold the two apart as much as it
draws them together, snaps; Ronald shouts something
abusive but indistinct at Marty, and flinging his hand up
behind him, lunges it forward, aiming for the boy's head
across the table. Marty dodges and escapes all but a flick
of the fingertip across his hair. But he gives a sharp pierc-
ing yelp of shock as he does so. Ronald is infuriated by
this evasion of his punishment. He seems bereft of all
sense not only of propriety but also of dignity, for now,
instead of cooling off and sending the boy out with a
sharp ticking off, he begins to stalk round the table after
Marty. The boy contrives to stay on the opposite side of
the table, but his normal pallor is now visibly increased
by fear.

There is a sound of movement in the next-door room.
Marty stops running and looks abruptly toward the door,
but Ronald hears neither the sound of the movement
nor the sound of the door opening. Nor, for an instant,
does he see the incredulous faces of Hilary and the other
half-dozen guests who have run to the source of the
scream that pierced into the drawing room, to be met by
the spectacle of their host with his back to them, dodging
from side to side in an effort to catch the little boy on
the other side of the table. But Ronald quickly senses
their presence, and turns about to face them. There is a
moment of silence; the guests have still not quite com-
prehended the meaning of what they behold. Ronald,
too, is trying to find a meaning for it, dazedly reliving
the evening in search of a clue. For a moment he has a
fancy that he can laugh the whole thing off—pretend

that he and Marty were only fooling around. But a look at the boy quickly tells him that this exit has been closed. There is something very peculiar in Marty's expression; the sheer whiteness of his face is now touched with an ominous green. Ronald notices that the boy is swallowing compulsively, and with a twinge of disgust, he realizes what is about to happen. He steps back, appalled, as Marty lurches forward, still looking intently at him, opens his mouth slowly as if making a huge, exaggerated smile, and then emits a miasma of yellow vomit that descends in a splatter across the dishes on the table.

There is a general gasp from the guests at the door, and Ronald turns away in despair from this final seal on the evening. He looks deflated and miserable, like a man who knows he has lost.

Hilary walks forward to her son and gently wipes around his mouth with a tissue. "Come on, dear, I'll take you home," she says to him. And taking his hand, she leads him out of the room, bowing her head and murmuring an almost inaudible apology to Ronald as she passes him.

The Bugle

D AVID DIDN'T RECOGNIZE the woman who opened the door to him when he arrived back at his parents' home.

She looked at him questioningly, awaiting an explanation.

"I'm David Pesketh. I think my parents are expecting me."

"Ah, yes. Come in."

He could smell smoke on her clothing as he passed by her into the hall. Her face, under crimped gray hair, was downward-inclined, forbidding.

"They were expecting you yesterday." There was a calm assurance about her that inhibited him from asking her directly who she was, and what she was doing here.

"I know they were. There was a strike in Tokyo. I'm very sorry." He wondered immediately why he had apologized to her. "Where are they now—are they in?"

"They're resting."

"I see. Well, I'll go up and say hello. . . ." He slid his two bulging suitcases into the shadowy alcove beneath the stairs. He was about halfway up when he heard her calm, flat voice again:

"They're asleep. I think you ought to wait. . . ."

He turned on the stairway and looked down at her, astonished. He had not seen his parents for three years.

"I don't think they'll mind, you know. . . ."

"No"—she looked directly up at him—"but they do need to rest."

He lingered a moment, registering the power of this stranger who was forcing him, after a minute's acquaintance, to appear churlish by proceeding or submissive by descending. It seemed oddly familiar, that dilemma, and associated somehow with the smells, brightnesses, and shadows of the house itself. And this familiarity in turn thrust him abruptly back into the long-untasted atmosphere of the place. He was home, back home.

He came down the stairs with a conciliatory smile.

"All right—I'll wait if you think that's best." He stood beside her, supposing that she would now volunteer some information about herself.

"I'll pour you a glass of milk" was all she said.

"Who are you—I mean, are you . . . are you staying here?"

"I live here." She looked at him a moment, her eyes unblinking. "You don't remember me, do you? I didn't think you would."

"*Remember* you?" He peered at her in the gloom of the large hall. The blue pigment of her eyes had all but crumbled into glazed dust, but what remained was of a tint again faintly familiar, again associated with the house itself.

"I'm Alice Cottle. I looked after you when you were small. Now I am looking after your parents."

"Ah . . . goodness . . ."

Alice Cottle . . . So she was back too. Miss Cottle the Confiscator, back home again, back before him, a spirit unbottled from the distillation of his childhood . . .

"It is strange, yes," she said, "but here I am, you

see. . . . Now you go in and I'll bring you a glass of milk." She walked briskly away.

"Actually I'll have a cup of tea," he called after her. "I'll make it myself."

She stopped, and paused a second in the corridor before turning to face him.

"We'll have tea in half an hour, when your parents come down."

David watched her turn and recede down the narrowing parallels of the corridor—tap tap tap . . .

He opened the living room door, then thought for a moment, and closed it without entering. He doubled back, and tiptoed up the stairs. Only when he reached the second landing, where his parents' bedroom was situated, did it strike him as laughable that he should feel he had to tiptoe up the stairs in his own home. He strode over to the bedroom door, knocked loudly once, and burst in with a cry of greeting.

There were dust sheets on everything. The great brass bed, the lacquered bamboo tables on either side of it, the plump little sofa by the window—all were shrouded in a pale gray drift of cloth.

The air was musty. Light billows of dust scudded away from his feet as he moved. He raised the sheet from an object beside him. It was the nutwood escritoire from which his mother had run her affairs. He tried the little drawers and hidden chambers that honeycombed its interior. They were all locked. A distinct feeling of weakness came over him. He crossed to the window. A large incinerator was smoldering on the back lawn, just where a japonica bush had been. The ground beneath it was scorched in a black circle.

A voice startled him:

"They don't sleep here any more."

She stood in the doorway with a glass of milk in her hand. David stared in shock at her a moment, then relaxed, and eased his collar from his neck.

"Ah. I see. That explains it. . . . Where are they, then?"

"On the first floor. They found the stairs too much. Your mother's in the blue guest room. Your father is in your room."

David sat—almost sank—down on the bed. It was like being told of a bereavement.

"It's all rather . . . odd." He freed his collar again. "Where do I sleep, then?"

"We thought the nursery. Most of the other rooms are closed up now, like this. I'm working on the attic rooms at the moment. There's a lot of rubbish to burn. Here—"

She handed him the glass of milk. He gulped it down. He could see her watching him as the last of the liquid slid into his mouth, her wrinkled face held bunched and contorted in the thick glass at the base of the tumbler. She put out her hand for the empty vessel.

"I'll wait for them downstairs," he said, wiping his lips.

The reunion at tea had an hallucinatory quality which David attributed to jet lag.

His father had seemed to move down the stairs with the leaden slowness of a shadow creeping round the calibrations of a sundial. His mother, who had been ill while he was away, had shrunk dramatically. She looked at him absently, her head half sunk in the shadow of her sweater's voluminous polo neck.

"It's lovely to have you back," she said. The words

reached him as if from an enormous distance, bereft of power.

There was a tinkle of porcelain as his father raised cup and saucer to lips with trembling hands.

"Tell us all about Japan," his mother said. "Was it like Thailand? No, you enjoyed Thailand. Where was the other place you were unhappy in? Peru, was it? Algeria?"

He felt acutely the judgment her confusion passed on the haphazard nature of his adult life. He had passed the same judgment himself, and sentenced the culprit to begin again, begin afresh.

"Japan is a very nice country. I've had enough of that way of life, that's all. It's galling to pass thirty and realize the only claim to distinction you have is the ability to teach your native tongue to foreigners. I could have been replaced by a box of cassettes. I probably have been by now. . . ."

Begin again. He knew about the state of affairs in England. The appointment of an American to dismantle the steel and coal industries had greatly tickled the Japanese businessmen he taught. One of them had compared it to a dishonored samurai blundering even in his self-disembowelment, and begging a former vassal to finish the job.

Even so, even so . . . In his dejection abroad, he had allowed himself to blur the idea of flying back across the world with that of leaping as swiftly into a new existence. There would be a space for him somewhere, a little gap in the margins of the economy, the shape of David Pesketh, and *voilà*, out of the plane he would step, and into the gap. . . .

He was tired, and went to bed early, but he was unable to sleep. He sat up and opened his eyes. As the dark of the big nursery receded, he could make out the dappled rocking horse in the corner, the children's books and annuals ranged by series on the bookshelf, their different sizes giving the outline a battlement effect. He could see the silhouette of a kangaroo squatting on the toy cupboard, a glint of moonlight in its glass eye. It was very strange to be among these things again. In their faint visibility, they formed the eerie picture that a device able to summon particles of light from the past might produce. A grainy, dreamy image no human hand could ever alter. He rose from bed and crossed to the window, drawing back the curtain. Abutting from the wall below him was the sloping glass-and-steel roof of a greenhouse, where his father had once cultivated tomatoes. He could see in the moonlight that it was empty now, and derelict. A faint glow came from the ashes of the incinerator on the lawn.

The days were warm and quiet. If he rose before nine, there would be a tinkling breakfast of crustless toast and tea. If later, nothing; Alice locked the pantry between mealtimes.

His mother wandered about the garden, pruning and digging. His father sometimes played patience, or leafed through an ancient copy of the *Illustrated London News*. Time distended itself immeasurably in the old man's presence. Vast flights of imagination could be accomplished between two ticks of the clock in the room where he sat snoozing in his high-backed chair, his eyes half open like an old dog's, a pool of cards under his limp hand.

Neither of them drove any longer. The car was still in the garage, but only Alice was insured. She went into town once a week, to do the shopping and have her hair done. The rest of the time she moved about the house, tidying, preparing meals, taking boxloads of junk from the attic rooms to feed the incinerator on the back lawn, standing immobile as a flurry of sparks rushed up before her. The smell of burning came and went on the breeze. Sometimes a moth-sized flake of ash was blown inside the house.

David could see her through the nursery window as he sat filling in application forms. She had found a chest full of old clothes. Flames gave way to thick white billows of smoke as she stuffed the wool, tweed, and cotton into the hot steel basket. She looked up at the nursery window, and David dropped his glance back down to the forms.

It wasn't long before letters began to arrive back for him. *We are sorry to have to inform you. We regret we are unable. I'm afraid we cannot. There were three four five thousand applications for the post. We were looking for a younger person. For someone with more relevant experience. We are sorry. We regret.*

The summer days grew long and slow.

He lay in bed watching smoke disperse from cumulus to cirrus to nothingness. Alice brought him a glass of milk. As he drank it, he remembered a childhood whim of leaving a half inch of liquid behind, in case the last mouthful should unveil a spider. "All of it up, now," Alice would say. White milk sluicing away from the black tangle of the creature, limbs bedraggled and awry like the stem of a tomato; tumbling onto his lips . . . *all of it up, now, all of it* . . . He drained the glass and handed it back to her.

By the time he had roused himself, she was back at the incinerator, cramming big objects from a tea chest into it. The sky was a heavy ocher, patched with dark

clouds; Alsatian colors. Tall flames with peacock greens
and blues in them streamed upward in front of her.
A table lamp disappeared into them, an enormous
book. . . . There was an abandon in her movements. She
took a black box from the tea chest and shoved it into
the fire. David watched it smolder and ignite. Through
the comb of flames devouring it, he could see the
wooden sides disintegrate. Peeping through burning
slats was something shiny and metallic. More charred
material fell away. The object was gold and curved. It
was the bell of a brass bugle. For a moment it shone out
brighter than the fire around it. Then gradually it tarnished, and blackened with soot.

There were forms to fill in, and letters of application
to compose. There was nothing else to do. He wrote his
name on a form. His hand was shaking violently, and
the letters came out malformed, like a child's. He let the
pen drop, and went to lie down on his bed. He stayed
quite still. Soon he was conscious of nothing but the
smell of burning.

"I hope we're not too quiet for you," his mother said at
lunch.

"I'm all right. I'll soon, you know . . ."

Minute nibbling sounds.

"Yes?" Alice said.

"Get something . . ."

There was a silence.

"You need cheering up!" his father exclaimed, surprised at the discovery. A moment later he announced
he had an idea.

"I'll get the projector out. We'll put up the screen in
the drawing room and make some popcorn like we used

to." He looked cautiously at Alice. She folded her napkin into its silver ring, and rose to her feet with the air of someone conscious of exercising magnificent self-control.

"I'll see to the dishes," she said, leaving the room.

There was some ancient popcorn in a jar at the back of the pantry. David attended to it, while his father ambled off to set up the cine show. He heated the oil with a few grains of corn in it. Alice was in the kitchen with him, washing the dishes. She made no attempt to speak to him as he stood by the saucepan waiting for the grains to explode. Nothing happened for a long time.

"Wouldn't you like to watch a film with us?" he asked, purely to break the silence. She didn't answer.

Pop pop pop.

"Your oil's ready," she said, without turning from the sink. "Please don't leave a mess."

"Don't worry. I'll clear it all up." He poured a cupful of grain and some sugar into the pan.

"Please do."

A hailstorm erupted under the heavy lid. The cartoon sound stirred residual memories: gleeful anticipation . . . excitement . . . a whiff of brilliant dreamtime. . . .

He took the pan off the heat, and lifted the lid to view the miraculous increase in its contents. The smell was shatteringly sweet. Shiny amber husks the shape of ladybird wings were splayed around the burst corn. He poured the golden mass into a bowl and carried it through to the drawing room.

The curtains were drawn. His mother turned to him in the gloom and patted the space on the sofa beside her. His father stood by the cumbersome projector, adjusting the angle of its beam until the square of light was flush with the four sides of the screen.

The two big spools revolved at a stately pace, whirring

like a ratchet. Blurred white numbers on a gray background counted down to zero. A brief tumult of flickering words and shapes followed, and suddenly they were
watching Charlie Chaplin eavesdrop on gold prospectors
in a Western saloon.

David sat back into the sofa, feeding himself popcorn,
surrendering to the grainy transmutations on the square
of light. Dust showed up in the white areas, hair-fine
coils and strands like broken watch springs.

He was comfortable in the darkness of the warm drawing room, listening to the whirring spools, the crunch of
popcorn. He was aware, in a peripheral way, of Alice
moving briskly about the house, opening and closing
doors, carrying boxes down from the attic. The activity
enhanced rather than disturbed the comfort of his enclosure, like rain on a car.

A villain fell over a precipice and plunged down into a
turbulent river that swept him away like a piece of flot-
sam. David chuckled.

"Ah, yes," his father said, standing up to flick a switch
on the projector. The river's flow reversed. The man
swirled back upstream, slid out of the water, and rock-
eted back up, to alight on the lip of the precipice.

David could see the illumined outline of his mother's
face bulge into a smile. She turned and patted his leg.
He leaned against her.

The film ended. Her father switched on the light and
took another reel from the box. They remained hushed
while he threaded it onto the projector, anxious not to
break the room's fragile spell. Footsteps thumped overhead.

It was a home movie. A card bearing the legend *Pesketh Films Inc.* wobbled on the screen, followed by another: *Tuscan Rhapsody.*

A stream of clouds seen from above through an airplane window. Mrs. Pesketh in a bright red dress gazing up at a cathedral front, her streaked blond hair half hidden in a silk scarf. Camera follows her gaze, giving a blurred, unsteady impression of stonework and statuary. Mr. Pesketh, tanned and dapper in a light summer suit, standing by a high stone balustrade looking out over vineyards and yellow hills tiered with olive trees. A breeze ruffles his hair. The scallop-shaped piazza at Siena milling with people. Scarlet and gold banners fluttering from balconies. Horses and riders in fantastical heraldic costume flash by. . . .

They sat bewitched. There were thundering sounds from above; a trunk or another tea chest being hauled down the attic stairs.

More clouds. David sat bolt upright. He remembered what was coming next.

A shot of the garden gate, and there he was in the porch, standing in front of Alice, her hands on his shoulders. He was in shorts and a T-shirt, and looked impossibly delicate. He was smiling into the camera.

Smiling directly at David, who drew in his breath and stared back at himself, electrified.

He shook off Alice's hands and ran forward over the bright green lawn. The camera followed him to his mother, who bent down to kiss him and handed him a little present, which he opened, his eyes alight with curiosity. It was a walnut. He peered at it bemusedly. His mother showed him a concealed button to press. The nut sprang open at its rim, and out of it poured a cascade of white silk embroidered with the gold and scarlet emblems of the Sienese banners.

"Ah, yes," Mr. Pesketh said, and stood up to flick the reverse-motion switch.

"No," David cried. . . .

The tumbled silk gathered itself up and disappeared inside the walnut, the hinged shell snapping shut behind it. The boy wrapped it up and handed it to his mother, embracing her. He ran backward across the lawn, back to the woman waiting in the doorway. Her hands came down onto his shoulders.

A while later, some family friends came with their daughter Lucy, his own age. She had ginger hair and blue eyes, a pollen of golden freckles scattered all over her face and arms. It was the first crush of David's life. The feelings she aroused in him were like amazing, invisible toys. He almost believed he could conjure them into visibility by making her laugh just a little louder at his clowning, goggle even wider at the feats of daring he performed for her. What would they look like if he could see them? Shimmering things dusted in gold.

They sat up in a tree, watching the yellow roses and lilac blossom turn luminous in the summer dusklight, the green of the lawn deepen. It was still light when Alice Cottle came to fetch them to bed. Lucy was put to sleep in the nursery, next door to his room. He crept in there when Alice had gone. They stood by the window. The noise of wood pigeons in the distance was like flute sounds bubbled through water. The chalky red flowers of a japonica bush took fire from the disappearing sun. They talked and giggled, louder and louder, breaking into snatches of songs they both knew, abandoning themselves. . . .

There was a sound of footsteps stomping into the corridor.

It gave the situation a new complexion: a thrill, but a peculiar, queasy sort of thrill. They heard Alice open the door of his room and call his name. He whispered to Lucy to get into bed and pretend she was asleep. He climbed out of the window, lowering himself onto a steel rib of the greenhouse roof, then dropped to the ground and slipped in through the door.

He stood trembling among the darkened foliage of the tomato plants. The thrill, the queasy thrill, was intensifying, not receding. Warm air, moist and sweet with the musk of the plants, enclosed him. He felt weightless, afloat. What was happening to him? His whole body was tingling. Clusters of new tomatoes dangled from the plants like the smallest, most secretive of baubles on a Christmas tree. They were tight and gold, some beginning to redden, so that the gold sheen was no more than a powdering. There were masses of them, gleaming faintly in what remained of the light. Was it from them, or from the rich air, or from the giggles of Lucy still ringing in his ears, or from inside himself, that this sweet tingling dizziness radiated? He played his hands through the plants, trailing his fingers around the hardsoft fruit, toying with them. A great pulse of sweetness traveled through him. He felt he was about to burst into some dazzling world of unimaginable power and pleasure.

He had to move. He stumbled out of the greenhouse. The air was cool, the zodiac freshly tattooed on the deep blue sky. He entered the house through the back door and ran up to his room. He stood there in a delirium of wonder, his heart racing. Euphoria was like a wild animal in him, struggling to break out. There was a black instrument case on the table. He opened it up and took from the blue plush of its interior his shiny brass bugle.

He put it to his lips, filled his lungs, and blasted a reveille onto the silent night.

He turned and she was there in the doorway as if summoned, her face taut and white, her hand outstretched:

"Give it to me."

Heart's Desire

The air thin and pure, danger near and the spirit full of a joyful wickedness; these things go well together.

I close my book. Nietzsche's heroics make me doubly uncomfortable in this place. The air is warm and thick, velvety with the smell of balsam that grows in dense tangles along the river's deep banks. There is no likelihood of danger.

Sharon lies beside me in the long dry grass, looking across to the village green, where a fete is in progress. Philip and Mandy are flirting with what they imagine to be great delicacy and wit. Mandy has pulled a balsam plant from the bank and is massaging the tips of the tense seed capsules to make them explode, to which minor natural phenomenon she responds with infantile glee.

The sky is solid blue. I glance at the sun, look away, close my eyes: a twisted rope of light glows on my retinas.

"Look, Philip, I can do it with my tongue," Mandy says.

He watches while she selects the most swollen seed capsule from the plant and dangles it in front of her opened lips. She slides out her tongue and begins to lick the sensitive surface of the capsule, looking coyly at

Philip as she does so. The thing bursts, and spatters her mouth with white and green seeds. She giggles, and turns over yieldingly beneath Philip who, roused by this performance, is inspired to kiss her.

"Those seeds are poisonous, you know," I tell them.

She pushes Philip off her and spits. I laugh. They look up to me because I know more at nineteen than they do at twenty-four or will at fifty-four. How contemptible they are! Look at them—Philip, mustached, in cheap sports clothes; Mandy in an outfit that struggles desperately to refer to every fashionable lifestyle from the past decade and falls, exhausted, into a senseless jumble of denim, leather, silk, and cheesecloth. They try to pass themselves off as sophisticates among their duller-witted peers. Philip has recently discovered irony and repartee, and is attempting to make a reputation as a wag; Mandy has a connection in town who supplies her with amphetamines, which she sells to us at cost price. Worst of all, they are getting married, and it is generally assumed that Sharon and I will do likewise, if only for the sake of symmetry.

"Teach me to roll a cigarette, Simon," she says to me. She regards these lessons, which she studiously fails to master, as a kind of publicly acceptable foreplay—a sensitization of the fingertips prior to their application, in private, elsewhere. She looks at me pleadingly. She has a mild, rubbery face that seems different every time I look at it. But these days it is always pleading, always close to tears. I feel a horrid neural shimmering ripple through me. At this moment the idea of intimacy with her is repellent. I ignore her and stand up to look at the fete.

There is a semicircle of white marquees bordered with bright pennants. A brass band in the center is playing a

Sousa march. The sound that reaches me is tinny, all
the resonance having been creamed off by the interven-
ing grass. The polished instruments fracture the sunlight
into minute sparkling reflections. I resist a brief impulse
to be charmed by this sight. I watch the villagers milling
among the stalls as if in this annual redistribution of
books, crockery, and junk each might find at last the
object of his heart's desire. I watch three solemn infants
slowly revolving on an old, hand-cranked merry-go-
round while a man misses a coconut three times and
another flings wet sponges into the face of an elderly
woman imprisoned in makeshift stocks. I crane forward
and look past the sandstone tower of the church to the
empty dovetailing fields that fan onward and outward to
the horizon. I imagine each field to be a year in my life,
and that unless the unimaginable descends upon me like
a gigantic bird of prey, to annihilate me, or bear me away
from this place, the years will disappear as eventlessly as
the fields.

We stroll over to the green. A master of ceremonies is
announcing the results of the car and lady competition:
"Mr. Desmond Wendigo with his immaculate 1925 Bent-
ley and his equally immaculate, I hope, wife, Janet, in
beautiful period costume complete with parasol, which
Janet tells me is made of real antique silk, not much
use in the rain I should think, but very lovely all the
same . . ."

"I'd rather fuck the car than the lady," Philip says with
a snigger.

I slip away. I wish evaporation on them all. What
atrocity did I commit in my past life, that I should have
been born into this stupefying dullness?

The afternoon heat has begun to slow things down. People are seeking refuge in the refreshment tents where urn-brewed tea and donated cakes are dispensed by well-dressed, well-spoken ladies thrilling to the curious pleasure of serving their social inferiors.

A few people continue to rummage among the stalls —flicking through old novels and magazines, fingering the ragged leaves of unsold geraniums—but their hearts are no longer in it. The elderly lady is still hanging in the stocks, though nobody can have thrown anything at her for a while, as her face and hair are quite dry. The merry-go-round and coconut shy have been abandoned. I find an empty chair and sit down. Little moves. Heat encloses the green. I feel like something rigid in a scene fixed in the dome of a huge glass paperweight. There is no wind: even the pliancy of the surrounding trees seems a dispelled illusion.

Thus it is that I glimpse three figures moving toward me from the roadside entrance to the fete. In the center is a tall girl with golden hair fastened on one side by an ornate clip; from the way it sparkles in the sun, it looks as if it is encrusted with diamonds. She is wearing a blue translucent silky dress, sleeveless, thigh-length, and held to her waist by a silvery belt. Her wrists are braceleted and her feet are bare. The young men on either side of her are slightly shorter. They are dressed in light summer suits with pleated trousers and loose jackets pinned back by wrists entombed in spacious pockets. One of them has a short crop of ginger hair, which he has accentuated by wearing a bright red tie. The other has a less distinguished look. His hair is a lifeless brown, and hangs in clusters around a large, moonish face, the only remarkable features of which are a pair of American-looking glasses. Judging from the action of the sunlight on them, they are bifocals. He has a mauve orchid in his buttonhole, and in place of a tie, a dimpled cravat. The three of them move toward me with the uninhibited, leisurely pace of animals that have no predators.

They take a brief interest in the stalls—seldom pausing, but casting an amused eye over whatever wares or entertainments offer themselves to their attention. They are laughing and talking loudly, unselfconsciously. I can hear the clear tones of their voices. As they approach me I begin to hear their words. "It's the same every year," the girl says as they amble past the merry-go-round. "They make a great fuss about it, trying to get us all to join in, then after a couple of hours they get bored stiff with it."

She pauses while the bespectacled young man drops a coin in a tin, picks a sponge out of a bucket of water, and throws it into the face of the elderly lady, who receives it without flinching.

"Still, it's harmless fun, I suppose, and they don't have much else to amuse themselves with. They get a bit livelier in the evening, though. If you like, we can eat at the pub restaurant tonight and watch them all getting drunk."

"That might be fun," says the ginger-haired boy.

"Yes, we'll treat you, Julia," says the other.

I recognize the girl, though I don't know her. Probably she belongs to one of the London families who own large weekend houses scattered about the village. I presume the boys are her guests. I admire the cool justice of her words. The sunlight radiates about her head in a nimbus of stray hairs. I feel an attraction to her—to all three of them. I will them to pause before me and say, with outstretched arms, "Come with us, Simon."

Of course, they continue right past me. They reach

the gateway to the fallow field adjacent to the fete. With a sweeping bow, the ginger-haired boy ushers his friends through the gate, and closes it behind himself. Laughing, they walk away along a deep-rutted track that leads through the grass and buttercups to the wood beyond.

They have hardly paused at all during their visit to the fete; have treated it like a pageant devised by well-meaning but clumsy artisans in the hope of entertaining a passing entourage of nobles.

I watch them as they approach the wood. A flock of swallows performs spectacularly coordinated swoops and gyrations above them. I turn back to the fete. Little stirs. Again I look at the three figures. They disappear into the wood, rolling away from me like fabulous creatures in an interrupted dream. I rise, and follow them.

On one side of the track the grass has been cut. It lies in pillowy drifts, giving off a sweet scent that rises with the heat from the warm earth. The wheel ruts along the path are floored with a mosaic of bleached and dried flakes of mud. The world is warm, still, and brittle. Everything is very clear. As I approach the wood I have the impression of being able to distinguish not only the individual leaves on the trees, but also the minute trees embossed on every leaf.

The wood itself is immediately cooler. Light filters greenly through the canopy of leaves, or falls here and there in slender shafts that redeem small insects and motes of dust from obscurity to a brief illumination. A few small flowers stand out among the decaying leaves like crystals in a dull rock. A clump of foxgloves cups an unfiltered beam of light in a dark pink chalice.

I follow the path through the wood, catching from time to time a glimpse of the girl's blue dress or a faint trace of laughter from one of the men. I have no plan. I listen to the satisfying crackle of my own footsteps, and to the whispery friction of birds moving among the leaves overhead.

I pass a steel-sheened lake and recall, from childhood poaching days, the whiff of fish slime, and the frantic death quiver of tiny muscles cupped in the palm. The perfect reflection of a fallen silver birch twins its branches into the double hemisphere of a brain, to which the wood with its quiet creatures and watery light might be no more than a figment of imagination.

The path ends at a gate through which I see my quarry disappear. I wait until the three are once more out of sight. I lift the latch of the gate and enter in.

It leads into an orchard abandoned to nettles and fireweed. On either side of the overgrown path stand rows of espaliered pear trees, lichened like monuments in a neglected cemetery. Through the wenned contortions of each entirely dead-looking limb, a few delicate leaves and some small pears have miraculously been extruded into the air.

The gate at the far end of the orchard is arched with a thick arbor of honeysuckle that gives me a stiflingly sweet lungful of scent as I pass beneath it. Stellar clusters of wild garlic stud the walkway beyond. There is an untrimmed hedge on one side—dog roses clinging to the yew, throttled in turn by crimson gorgets of some opulent parasite. White trumpets of convolvulus wind themselves in and out among the buds and blooms, and over it all sparkle the gossamer weavings of spiders waiting patiently in the shadows of the leaves.

On the other side of the walkway is a wall, over the top of which I can see the tiled roofs of three successively larger outhouses, and beyond them three ornate brickwork chimneys jutting jaggedly into the blue air.

The metallic scratching of a key being fitted into a lock reaches me from where the path disappears behind a large tangle of rhododendrons. I halt until I hear the muffled slam of the door. I look about me and begin to take in the loveliness of this place. I have no inclination to leave it, as I know I should.

Through the broken slats of a wooden door in the wall, I can see a large lawn reaching to the outhouses, and round to a bay-windowed promontory of the house itself. I put my hand to the door. The wood is warm and makes a dry creaking as I push it open. I enter and stand in the shadow of the wall. I can feel my heart beating. The lawn is bordered with shrubs and rose trees in full bloom. Between them and the surrounding wall a path leads round to a kitchen garden ending at a large box hedge, in which the vestiges of some sort of topiary show as a dark form beneath a mass of unkempt stalks. On the ground beyond that is a small, dark, but shiny object looking like a molehill that has been glazed by the summer's incessant heat, and just beyond that is the bay window, set into soot-black bricks embered with blooms of maiden's blush.

I begin to creep slowly and quietly round the half-concealed path. I reach the kitchen garden and pause by a plot of herbs, trying to calm myself while still hidden from the window by the box hedge. There are big furry bees hovering around the herbs, purring like kittens. I can distinguish thyme and rosemary in the air, and lico-rice. Fennel plants stand in tall clusters by the hedge, the juncture of each blue-green stalk ribbed and bellied like a lute.

I peer cautiously around the hedge. The first thing I see is the glazed molehill, only it is a tortoise lying peace-fully asleep, its wizened face half-retracted into the shade of its shell. How I should like to lie down as tranquilly in this place . . . but I have things to do.

I edge myself around till I stand in full view of the bay window. It looks into a large drawing room—too large and lofty to seem cluttered, but nevertheless abundantly filled with objects. There are tall, glass-fronted bookcases lining the three walls. The wood at the top of each is carved in symmetrical wave patterns, and the sinuous motif is echoed all about the room by peacock feathers fanning out from the slender necks of blue and yellow ceramic pots, and by the huge curving leaves of a lush tropical plant resting on a lacquerwork cabinet. Sofas with ruffled antimacassars, a brick fireplace with blackened tongs and pokers, vast gilt-framed mirrors shaped like lyres—too tarnished to be of service to vanity—old Persian rugs, faded, but sufficiently colored to recall a splendor that no longer needs to be proclaimed so forcibly . . . A room that has subsided through generations to a perfect equanimity.

I extend that equanimity to the room's absent occupants. How could a person live in such surroundings and not emerge with spaciousness of mind, tolerance, composure? These are qualities I desire for myself. I feel excluded from them by barriers as transpicuous but impenetrable as this bay window. I cannot acquire them any more than my own home with its brassy little rooms all patchworked in greasy linoleum and sickly wallpaper could suddenly acquire the grace of this house. It is unjust, but it is not the injustice I resent. Every virtue depends for its existence on its opposite; I know this. Poverty of intellect, emotion, and imagination are as integral to the ordering of human life as material poverty. Most people experience this fourfold poverty so that the notion of superabundant delight can be kept alive by at

least a few. The destitute live in numb contentment because the nature of their poverty makes it impossible for
them to conceive of any larger form of existence than
their own, or not with any conviction.

So much for them, but by a quirk of nature there are
some individuals in whom appetite has failed to adjust to
circumstance. These people live in a continual aching
state of desire, born from a certainty that they were as-
signed the wrong body, the wrong personality, the wrong
life, through a gross bureaucratic blunder on the part of
the Fates. It is like being a transsexual, only they have
the operation, and we have nothing but dreaming. I
have no precise picture of my birthright, but the sight of
this window's ghostly reflection of myself, hovering
among the objects in the room, seems to taunt me with
my loss, to rub salt into the wounds of my dispossession.

A strip of sunlight appears like an unfurled carpet on
the floor to one side of the room. I stand quite still and
hold my breath. I am aware of my own presence like a
speck of dirt on the scene. But as the girl Julia and her
friends enter along the strip of sunlight, all three of them
talking loudly and simultaneously, a transistor blaring in
the hands of the ginger-haired boy, I begin to feel this
self-consciousness not disappear but dwindle to the in-
significance of a man walking backward in a train that is
rushing him forward.

As she walks toward the center of the room, the girl
begins to shuffle her steps and snap her fingers, making
a Creole dance that syncopates to the beat coming from
the radio. Her blue silky dress shimmers, and her bracelets flash in the sunlight. She stands on the hearth rug,
swaying and snapping her fingers, smiling mock-
flirtatiously at the two men, who smile back with barely
concealed lust. I share their hunger; I can visualize my-

self and Julia caressing each other on a large soft bed, and I see it as something that must happen as a matter of course. But my desire encompasses more than Julia; I want to distribute myself among the three of them, among all the contents of the room. . . .

The sound of a jet crossing the sky overhead deflects Julia's attention from her friends to the window. As she looks down from the sky, her eyes rest in transit dreamily on my own. A second later she flinches as she registers my presence, and I am running.

I sprint straight across the lawn, push through the dilapidated door, down the hedged walkway, under the honeysuckle arbor, past the espaliered pear trees, out the back gate, down into the wood, past the lake, on and on as fast as I can along the flower-bordered path . . . I arrive panting at the fallow field next to the fete.

Less fear than exhilaration makes me run. I have been granted a glimpse of something; a vigor on which I can coast. Breath pours into my lungs like gouts of molten metal. I feel a fierce ebullience ascend to take control over me. It promises me ruthlessness, the ability to make events ancillary to my desires. I feel capable of doing anything. Most immediately I feel I can extort some money from my parents so that I can dine tonight at the pub restaurant where, if they do as I heard them say, Julia and her friends will be.

I turn down along the road that leads to the housing estate where my parents conceived and bred me. A spruce patch of grass lies like a bib before the yellow-brick houses.

There is a light on in the kitchen.

"Who's there?" a man's voice snaps. I feel my stomach acidulating as I hear it.

"Who d'you think?" I say.

My father is at the table, tinkering with an iron. He has written me off as a good-for-nothing. His nose is shaped like a shoe and sticks out with flagrant disregard for facial symmetry. It is difficult to take him seriously, yet this forcibly retired mechanic can be quite merciless in his own way. He mutters something disparaging and turns back to the iron.

My mother, sitting opposite him, casts her eyes down to the tartan-papered kitchen table on which is spread a heterogeneous set of tea crockery. Then she peeps up toward me. Catching my eye, she makes an expression I interpret as begging my forgiveness for her choice of husband, and by extension, for their having failed me utterly as parents. I smile back at her. The room smells faintly of gas and rancid butter. The morning's splash of milk from the fridge is souring on a violet square in the checked linoleum. Walls blister through a crust of yellow paint.

"I need some money," I say. "I'm going to the Royal Oak restaurant." I have in mind a beautiful lie that will certainly make them deliver.

"You don't get a penny out of me nor your mother neither," my father says with manufactured anger concealing a delight in obstruction. "You want to waste money in restaurants, you get a job and pay for it. No, Jen, not over my dead body. He's a bloody layabout. And an ess en o be too."

I produce my lie: "I'm going to propose to Sharon. I think I should take her out to dinner first."

Two crumpled notes are swiftly produced from an old beige purse, and as I turn to leave the room, a bluebottle, materializing from nowhere, meets its maker beneath my father's yellow palm.

Venus and a thumbprint moon are silver and amber in the evening sky, and the air is mellow, as I click the door behind me. The yellow-green corn on either side of the road looks more mineral than vegetable, wire strands from the vast circuit grid of some ethereal machine. A pipistrell darts from the cone of an oast house by the river, and down in the water thick tresses of weed show green and red through the glassy currents that comb them downstream.

The forecourt of the pub is lit with red and yellow fairy lights and a single piercingly bright kerosene lamp. Men and women in shirtsleeves and light cardigans are laughing and drinking calmly at the trestle tables. Here and there the glow of a pipe bowl or a cigarette reaches me through the twilight, and as I draw nearer I can discern the powdery blues and pinks of hydrangeas fringing the tables in striped tubs. The scene is seductive, the life I am preparing to abandon concentrating all its sweetnesses in an effort to seduce me back. From the woods beyond, there comes suddenly the rippling song of wood pigeons ushering in the night. I remember a phrase: *a little slumber, a little folding of the hands to sleep.*

But there by the trellised entrance to the public bar is Philip, with his pretentious mustache arching and contracting like a traumatized slug as he regales a group of less loquacious villagers with some specimen of his laborious wit. And there, standing slightly apart from the group, is Sharon, stupidly confident behind her wounded face that her sweetheart will eventually arrive and heal her.

I slip past them unnoticed, and go into the restaurant.

There are fewer than a dozen tables, all laid with candle-lit glass and silver, empty except for one where an elderly couple are sipping soup in austere silence. Pink lamps hang from the walls, shedding dim light on the maroon carpet. Here I am. The couple nod at me faintly, acknowledging the fact. A waitress in black and white appears and looks at me in disbelief; I recognize her face from college.

"What do *you* want?" she says, and continues to attend to me with a studied parody of servility, furiously scribbling my order as if intent on immortalizing my every syllable as I utter it.

"I'll have the artichoke and then the . . . the *truite aux* . . . " I cannot bring myself to say it to her. "The trout."

"Any vegetable, sir?"

"Yes, bring me potatoes, and the baby courgettes, and the garden peas."

"The garden peas," she echoes.

"And a bottle of red wine. House red." I'll get a little drunk, I decide, before they come.

She brings me, presently, a spiky artichoke, and a gold dish of melted butter, then retreats to the doorway, where she stands watching me with insolent skepticism. I begin to dismantle the artichoke, realizing it is not a good choice for a solitary diner in a silent restaurant. The couple watch me absently as I pluck and dip, tooth out the flesh, and discard the leathery leaves. A sudden amplification of voices from the public bar next door launches the villagers into a new phase of their revelry. Carefully I sever the mosque dome of fibers from the disappointingly shallow basin of flesh.

Where is Julia? Why have they not come? The door

opens, but it is a drab threesome, who sit in the corner and behave themselves.

The elderly couple begin to assemble some anecdote from their past. They speak formally and listen politely to one another before making their own contribution. A stray piece of green food hangs from the man's lower lip. His wife cannot take her eyes from it, but lovingly resists pointing it out.

I swivel the homunculus that stares at me from the back of a polished spoon. I feel myself slipping toward melancholy. My sense of complete power appears to be deserting me like a drug wearing off. I have become aware of a jukebox playing in the bar next door. It makes me feel morbid; I imagine a heavy sliver of ceiling falling and slicing me in two, or a lunatic appearing at the door with a shotgun and blowing off my head. Where is Julia? And what difference will her presence make? I tip back the final sedimented drops of wine. The waitress brings a trout in an oval garden, and I order another bottle.

I toy with the blanched eye of the trout. Where are they? I think of the story of a genie held so long in a bottle that instead of being eternally grateful to its liberators, it curses them for not having turned up earlier. I lay down the heavy cutlery and feed myself peas, one by one, with my fingers.

A clamor of voices comes through the door, and here they are at last before me, vibrant and exuberant, twitching the drowsy room into life. The men are still wearing the same suits, but Julia has changed into a scarlet crepe dress thickly embroidered with gold thread, that hangs from her left shoulder, slashing downward to the opposite midriff, covering, but barely, the nipple of her right breast on its way. Two pink chrome umbrellas hang from her ears, and on her head is a black pillbox hat with a pinned-back veil and, in place of a plume, a little posy of yellow cinquefoil and checked fritillary. Her eyes are rimmed with kohl, her lipstick is mauve, the nails of fingers and toes are deep crimson. The apparel is faintly ridiculous, especially here, but she knows this, and stares challengingly at each face in the room. A widening of the kohl-rimmed eyes tells me she recognizes me, but she pretends she hasn't, and continues talking loudly with her friends.

They sit two tables in front of me, and from this proximity I observe their half-drunk performance.

"But, Ralph, how did you survive so long without alcohol?" Julia says.

Ralph, the bespectacled one, mimes a dog panting with thirst, then answers, "Actually, you can get anything you want in a Muslim country if you work in oil and you're white."

"It always amazes me how much of the world is Muslim," Julia says laconically. "Four million alone in—where was it?—Jakarta, I read somewhere." The drab threesome and the elderly couple are silent, listening.

"Well, two million, really," says Ralph, "if you take into account they're half the size of normal people." He laughs at his joke, and then, sensing disapproval gathering among the other diners, adds: "Still, I'm sure they're frightfully clever and aggressive and, ah, everything."

"I can't imagine anything worse than two million clever little aggressive Muslims, let alone four," says Julia.

"God no! What a thought," Ralph says, "not that we're racists or anything." He pauses mock-solemnly, while up into his wide, prematurely mottled face froths once more his irrepressible humor: "It's just that we can't stand wogs, yids, niggers, or micks!" It is too much for him. He neighs and snorts until tears come into his face. The elderly couple signal to the waitress for their bill.

The ginger-haired boy grins weakly at Julia. He is clearly too drunk to make much conversation, and too good-looking to need to. His beautiful pale blue eyes wander from her face to her half-exposed right breast, willing the scarlet crepe to slip.

Ralph orders more wine. "God, I'm drunk," he says. "Still, what the hell? Julia, you're looking *ravishing*, or have I already said that? Guy, stop looking at her so *obscenely*." He chucks Guy under the chin. "You're so good-looking, dear, you ought to start a sperm bank." Guy grins, and Ralph pours them all a glass of wine.

The elderly couple once more signal for their bill. I am struggling against a sensation I do not wish to acknowledge. I attack the mess on my plate, nearly choking on a bone in an effort to keep the sensation at bay.

"Talking of obscenities," Ralph says, "I bumped into that revolting girl we trussed up at the ball last year. She didn't know who I was, thank God, or I'd have been dead as this duck." More laughter, and a forkful of the duck displayed to the company.

"What girl was that?" Julia asks.

"Oh, you tell her, Guy." Guy begins to, but Ralph interrupts him and Guy sits back, grinning weakly and chuckling.

"You know, that disgusting fat lesbian with the huge Adam's apple who used to sit in Crooks shoveling beans into herself and plotting feminist *putsches* with her equally disgusting lezzy friends. You know the one— Eartha or Brunhild or something. . . ."

"Oh, I know this story," says Julia. She looks around the room with a curiously apologetic expression. Ralph, as she has guessed, is going to tell the story anyway.

"Nick Alton and a couple of his welder friends heard she'd got a ticket for being on the entertainments committee or something, so they roped me and Guy into this excellent plan. . . . Anyway"—Ralph begins to gnaw at a duck bone—"they got a car battery and some cheese wire and a piece of rope—oh, and also five black hoods with eye slits and things—all in a little suitcase. One of them kept an eye on the girl until he got her on her own, then he told her she was wanted urgently in the quiet room. Back he comes like greased lightning, and there we all are, waiting for her in our black hoods with all the wire and stuff, and a tray full of cocktail canapés."

He stops suddenly, as if his relish for the tale has abruptly drained away. Looking despondently at the torn flesh and cartilage on his duck bone, he says quietly, "Well, you know the rest. . . ."

Guy looks at him with a mischievous smile and chuckles a low, gravelly chuckle. Ralph catches the look, and the amusement; it seems swiftly to restore his vanished energy. He starts to chuckle himself, at first sardonically, as if at something grim, then by degrees more wholeheartedly, until he is laughing uncontrollably, his flabby frame quivering with delight, and he has once more to lift his glasses to wipe the moisture from his eyes.

"God, it was funny, though," he chortles. "Every time she"—but laughter chokes him—"every time she swallowed a canapé, her great big Adam's apple touched the cheese wire and she jerked back from the electric shock and her eyebrows went up and down like this, then when she wouldn't open her mouth we shocked her anyway, and when she did she couldn't resist swallowing all that lovely food. God, she was gross. We left her shedding tears from her little piggy eyes."

He wipes his face and sniffs. "Ah, dear," he says, descending from falsetto. "Pretty beastly thing to do, I suppose, but she never found out who it was." He empties his glass and adds, "Taught her a jolly good lesson anyway."

I find myself wondering what Sharon is thinking, waiting for me to show up at the bar. I am glad she is not with me.

"From what I hear, though," Ralph says, leaning conspiratorially toward the other two, "that wasn't the only funny thing happening at the ball." He tries to lower his voice, but his natural resonance makes the attempt futile. "Wasn't it you, Guy, who told me about some private little party a couple of the eights had going in another of those quiet rooms?"

Guy denies it, but giggles nervously, pushing a hand through his ginger hair.

"Yes, it was you, Guy; I may be drunk, but I remember distinctly. You'll love this one, Julia. They had this big, big table with a huge tablecloth going down to the floor, and under the table was a girl"—he manages at last a croaking, salacious hiss—"sucking them off as they ate. Ha! Ha! Ha! Can you *believe* it?" He quaffs at his wine. "They had a game going where they had to guess who was really having it done and who was faking it, or something, then some fellow wandered in by mistake, so they offered him a drink and pulled up a chair for him. . . ." He snorts, and gestures that they can guess what followed.

Julia rises and excuses herself. She has not looked entirely comfortable during this story, and as she stands up a hint of weariness all but dissolves the panache that carried off the risqué dress and the pillbox hat, so that she appears now awkward and frail.

"Idiot," Guy says with a smirk when Julia has gone.

"What d'you mean?"

"That girl under the table . . . didn't you know? Everyone says it was Julia."

"Oh, crap," Ralph says with a dismissive wave of his cigar. But before long a duet of bucolic laughter once more rises in a trumpeting crescendo. The waitress finally releases the elderly couple.

Julia returns to her companions, who are now puffing cigars. Ralph stares, as if reappraising her, through the lower meniscus of his bifocals. His face has slackened perceptibly from the wine.

"I'm very drunk, Julia," he says studiedly. "I couldn't possibly drive us back in the state I'm in."

"Well, we can walk through the woods."

"Yes, except that our cases and things are still in the car." The butt of his cigar glows brightly through its ruff of ash. "Listen, why don't we have a dip in that weir you were telling us about? That would freshen us up." He elaborates the proposal. Guy seconds it. Julia seems reluctant, but even more reluctant to forsake her insouciant style with a display of killjoy caution.

"I don't feel like swimming myself. But you can if you like . . ." she says.

My mind clear, my body drunk, I wade through the liquid red light of the room, and pay. The waitress thanks me sarcastically for my small tip, as if I have handed her something nasty in the classroom.

Villagers, drunk and rowdy, are beginning to stumble out of the bar into the scarcely cooler evening air.

I run down to the river, cross it, and stumble in darkness through the tangled balsam and dead nettles along its bank until I reach the weir.

It hardly merits that title, being a drop in level of less than two feet. The white rush of water falls into a black pool about thirty feet across, where people come to bathe in summer.

Waiting for them again, on the exposed root of an oak tree, I begin to feel calm. A breath of night breeze brings from the falling water a cool spray as fresh and delicate as the scent atomized from the pierced zest of a lemon. Ripples crested with moonlight play across the surface of the pool, and overhead the jagged silhouettes of trees are stenciled black against the sky.

The sound of Ralph's laugh comes from the opposite bank. I make myself invisible in the shadow of my oak tree. They sit down on an apron of grass that juts into the pool. Ralph jerks at his laces, throws off his shoes, stands up, and takes off the rest of his clothes. He looks like a large white jelly in the moonlight.

"What an Adonis I am, eh?" he says, and flops into the water. "Come on, you two," he shouts. "It's gorgeous." Guy begins to undress fastidiously, folding his clothes as he takes them off. He hovers naked in front of Julia, giggles drunkenly, and then climbs tentatively into the pool. They shout, and splash one another. Ralph plunges underwater, then erupts behind Guy, and tries to duck him. Guy turns and struggles for a moment, then yields to Ralph's grip, as if to a lover's embrace. Ralph lets him go, and shouts to Julia, who is sitting fully clothed on the bank, "Come on in, Julia, you'll love it." He splashes her.

"No, I don't feel like it. And please don't splash me."

"Now come on. Don't be a spoilsport."

"No, Ralph, I really don't want to."

Ralph swims up next to Guy and whispers something in his ear. They drift apart and float, separately, toward the bank. Then suddenly Ralph yells, "Get her."

They clamber out of the pool and close in on top of Julia, bringing her down as she begins, alarmed, to climb to her feet. Laughing loudly, they pin her to the ground.

"What are you bloody doing?" she cries out.

"We're going to throw you in." Ralph says it singsong, like a nasty child.

"Oh, don't be silly. . . ." She struggles, but Ralph sits astride her stomach and Guy crouches behind her, pinning her wrists above her head.

"Now how do we get this dress off?"

I watch from my hiding place as Ralph unties the single strap from Julia's shoulder and carefully pulls the dress over her breasts. I hear Julia scream and Ralph tell Guy to clap his hand over her mouth. I watch her kicking her legs and arcing her back so that, inadvertently, she allows Ralph to pull both dress and panties down to her ankles in one swift movement, revealing her white supple body wrestling naked beneath his haunches. Her pillbox hat lies crumpled northwest of her golden hair. Her cries come muffled through Guy's ineffectually placed hand. "Please get off me, please. I don't want to do this."

As Ralph turns to pull off her sandals, I realize, from what stands swollen above his water-shriveled scrotum, exactly what it is Julia does not want to do.

Ralph begins to prize her legs apart. "Look what you've done to me, my lovely friend," he says. "You really asked for this. Didn't she, Guy?"

Guy is giggling again, one hand on Julia's mouth, the other mauling her breasts.

I rise slowly to my feet. A peculiar sense of power

ascends through me as I stand looking down on this tangle of carrion, its fate at my disposal. Guy yanks his hand back from Julia's mouth: she must have bitten it.

"You pigs," she screams. "What d'you think I am?"

"The girl who sucked off two boat crews, that's what," Ralph says with a chuckle as he starts to wedge himself between her thighs.

"You're mad," she shouts, and begins to sob.

Enough, I decide. I pick up a large, flat stone from between the roots of the oak tree, and hurl it as hard as I can into the water, where it makes a formidable splash. The effect is instantaneous. Ralph leaps out from between Julia's thighs and crouches, peering from the bank, grabbing the pillbox hat to cover his buckling tumescence.

"Shit," he says. "What was that?"

Guy also flinches backward, and even Julia lies still and quiet for a moment.

"Who's there?" Ralph's shaky voice comes over the water. He reaches behind him for his glasses and peers into the shadows. He looks comical, crouching and swaying like a caged baboon squinting through its bars. I toss another stone into the pool.

"Voyeur," Ralph rasps at the void, then, changing his tone, says, "Nothing serious, whoever you are; just fooling around. Isn't that right, Julia?"

I send a handful of pebbles exploding onto the water.

"Christ! Let's get out of here, Guy." They bundle themselves into their suits, increasingly frenzied as I, laughing to myself, continue to pepper the water with stones. Julia is moaning quietly, and struggling back into her dress.

"Sorry, Julia," Ralph mutters. "Got a bit carried away. Still, no harm done, eh?"

"Go away," she sobs, "go away."

"We're going," says Ralph.

"Bye bye," says Guy. They disappear back toward the pub.

Alone, Julia kneels forward and looks into the wooded darkness on my bank.

"Who's there?" she asks. I remain silent, looking down on her as she uncrumples her hat and places it on her disheveled hair. A cool spray reaches my cheeks again. I creep back to the path and head home.

Heart's desire . . . I find myself smiling, as if I have witnessed not my own but someone else's will crumbling.

The kitchen light is on, and there at the table is my mother in a quilted nylon dressing gown, sipping tea.

"I waited up for you, dear. What did she say?"

For a moment I wonder what on earth she is talking about. Then I remember my lie.

"Oh," I say. "She accepted."

"I knew she would." My mother smiles indulgently and strokes my hair. "You were made for each other."